THE CASE OF THE POISONED PUMPKIN PIE

A PARANORMAL COZY MYSTERY

GHOSTLY GLENWOOD MYSTERIES

B I SKINNER

CONTENTS

ONE

A SLICE OF PARANORMAL LIFE

"I'm so excited! It's my favorite time of year!" Clara, my 145-year-old pink flannel nightgown wearing roommate, clapped her ghostly hands with glee.

"What's so good about it?" Mystery, our talking ghost cat responded.

"What's so good about it? Where do I start?" Clara said, her eyes twinkling. "There's a crisp magic in the air, don't you think? Leaves turning amber and gold, the comforting scent of wood smoke and spiced cider everywhere, cozy evenings spent reading by the fire, pumpkin-flavored everything, Halloween mysteries, Thanksgiving preparations, ohhh, it feels like *anything* could happen. And don't forget there's the Great Harvest Pie Showdown!"

Clara was so excited, if she weren't a ghost, I'd say her cheeks were flushed. Although I wish she wouldn't say that *anything* could happen. In my experience, that was just inviting trouble.

"Ohhh yeah, and it's mouse season!" Mystery exclaimed, rubbing her luminescent paws together like some kind of evil genius just waiting to take advantage of a helpless mouse.

"Mouse season?" I responded.

"Yesss," she hissed with a gleam in her eye. "When the air turns chilly, the mice come inside to get warm, then rock 'em, sock 'em, blammo!" She threw her paws through the air like she was punching out mice left and right.

"There are no mice in this house!" I exclaimed.

"Of course not, you have me," she grumbled, puffing out her fluffy chest.

I didn't know the house was haunted when I bought it after moving to Glenwood Springs from Jupiter, Florida. And I admit I said some very unflattering things when I spotted Clara in the window after the listing agent handed me the keys, and it was too late to back out.

But if I thought I was startled by Clara, that was nothing compared to when I met Mystery. As a ghost whisperer or Spirit Communicator, to use the formal term, I'd seen plenty of ghosts in my day. But when I realized that Mystery was talking, I had to sit down, I was so stunned. We didn't know how old Mystery was in ghost years. We only knew that, at some point, she finally used up the last of her nine lives.

Mystery and Clara weren't the roommates I would have asked for, but it turned out they were exactly the roommates, or family as I now thought of them, that I needed. Clara told me she remembered going to bed one night at the tender age of 93 with a glass of water and a book on her nightstand. Next thing she knew, her house was full of mourners and casseroles.

She admitted she saw the light and assumed she was supposed to cross over but was simply too busy to do so.Eventually, the light faded, and then it went out entirely, and that was how she still lived here.

Like most spirits, Mystery and Clara are tethered to the property where they died. However, unlike most spirits, they could leave the property in the bright pink, fully restored vintage VW bus the previous owners left behind when they moved out. Why would they leave behind something they worked so hard to restore? Because they were convinced it and the house were haunted. And they were right.

I didn't want *any* of it at first. Yet, here I am. Clara and Mystery are the family I haven't had since my parents and husband died, and whenever I drive the pink bus, everyone waves at me like I'm in a parade. Wouldn't they be shocked to learn it was me and two ghosts!

"Okay, you two, I'm going to swim, and then I'm off to the bakery. Juliet wants us to taste-test some pies she's working on. You want to come with?"

Clara shook her head. "No, dear. We made plans to binge-watch Real Housewives. The latest season just dropped, you know. Be sure to leave the TV on before you go," she reminded me. "Oh, and say hello to Harold for me."

Harold was a ghost who lived in the Hot Springs pool after drowning in it in 1902. And yes, my spirit roommates loved to watch television. I have lived an interesting life since moving to Colorado.

After my Army Ranger husband was killed in combat, and I got fired from my job as a cyber security consultant for losing my temper one too many times, I moved to Glenwood Springs, a small mountain town known for its one-of-a-kind mammoth hot springs pools and breathtaking scenery. I chose this town because I was sure it would be drama-free.

Yet my life here had been anything but drama-free. But

with Clara and Mystery, plus my best friends Juliet and Wendy, I've known more love and family loyalty than I could have ever imagined, and I wouldn't trade it for the world. Not even for a so-called drama-free life.

Sure, I could do with fewer dead bodies and stolen artifacts, but I had grown to love my friends and roommates fiercely. Besides, it had been quite a while since I came across any bodies, and I hoped that meant things had finally settled down. My work as a Paranormal Private Investigator was somewhat mundane lately, which was fine with me. Only last week, a woman hired me to convince the ghost who was constantly scratching on the side of her house to please knock it off. But it wasn't a ghost. It was the neighbor's out-of-control tree branches. When I pointed that out, she admitted it only happened when it was windy.

I headed to the Hot Springs to swim my usual laps, already dreaming about the delicious pie I'd taste later. I bought a yearly membership pass to the pool after meeting Juliet because having a best friend who owned a bakery wasn't as great as a person would think. Sure, it was like having a golden ticket to a world of sweet surprises—a constant source of freshly baked goodies to satisfy my cravings whenever I wanted. But it was also why I had to work so hard to burn all those extra calories!

As I drove down North River Street, I honked and waved at John, the ghost who always rode his bicycle along this stretch of road. A few minutes later, I pulled the pink bus into my usual parking spot and headed for the lobby doors. Ethan, a tall, lanky college student studying chemistry at Colorado Mountain College, was in his usual spot at the front desk.

"Morning, Holly!" he greeted me with a cheerful wave.

"Hey, Ethan!" I responded, adjusting my swim gear bag

on my shoulder before scanning my membership card over the reader. "Any exciting plans for this afternoon?"

"Just a hike up to Hanging Lake with some friends," he replied, then added with a grin, "are you excited about the pie-baking competition?"

"As a matter of fact, after I finish here, I get to taste test pumpkin pies at Sol Conceptions!" I bragged.

"Ohhh man, I wish my best friend owned a bakery," he said wistfully.

"It definitely has its perks," I admitted on my way to the locker room.

I quickly changed into my swimsuit, tied back my long dark hair, slipped into my flip-flops, and wandered out to the pool area. As usual, the pool was quiet at 9:00 on a Saturday morning in late October. And if you were picturing your standard, run-of-the-mill lap pool, you'd be mistaken. Hugely mistaken.

Glenwood Springs, Colorado, was home to the world's largest year-round, outdoor hot springs pool. Last year, Juliet, Wendy, and I came on Christmas Day, and it was magical. We spent the morning relaxing in the Therapy Pool, surrounded by majestic mountain peaks stretching to the sky, their rugged silhouettes blanketed by a fresh layer of pristine snow. As we soaked blissfully in the therapeutic waters, lazy snowflakes drifted down from a pearl-gray sky, dancing on the light breeze while steam rose from the water's surface, creating a misty veil. I still get chills remembering it. What an extraordinary place to live.

They recently expanded the resort by five additional pools, some with water fountains. The original Grand Pool (which I liked to call the warm pool), where I swam laps, was two city blocks long and naturally heated at around 90 degrees. The Therapy Pool (I called it the hot pool) was 104 degrees. No lap swimming in that one. Just relaxing.

I spent around thirty minutes swimming laps (no sign of Harold) before my painfully stiff left shoulder got the best of me, so I wandered over to the Therapy Pool to soak in a bubble chair, which was almost like sitting in my own personal hot tub when a little girl pointed at me.

"Whoa! Mom!" she said as she and her mother walked past me. "Did you see that lady's eyes? They're purple!" she exclaimed.

"Now, Larisa, that's not polite!" her mother scolded.

"They're lavender," I muttered, resisting the urge to stick my tongue out at her. I got that all the time. It was especially hard when I was a kid, and the others bullied me over it. As a child, it definitely didn't help that I saw dead people. And lived in a foster home. Ah well, what could I do? People were curious. I would have had some choice words for the girl in the past, but I was working on my quick temper. Juliet and Wendy were the first friends I ever had who actually called me out on it in a loving but firm way.

After a brief soak in the Therapy Pool, my shoulder loosened up, and I headed back to the locker room to shower and change. But as I left, I had to dig through my swim bag for my keys.

"Dangit, where are they?" I mumbled, feeling around on the bottom of the bag, not watching where I was going. From out of nowhere, a hulking figure knocked into me so hard the impact sent me sprawling onto the wet tile floor, spilling the contents from my bag all around me. Before I could even catch my breath, the man who'd knocked me down glared at me and groused, "Watch where you're going, lady!" then stomped off without offering to help, leaving me stunned and irritated on the floor.

"Holly! Are you okay?" Ethan exclaimed, rushing to my side to help me to my feet.

"Yeah, I guess so," I said, brushing myself off while collecting my things scattered on the floor. And they said *I* had a temper! "What's that guy's problem? And why does he look familiar?"

"Are you serious? That's Sebastian LeClair, the famous TV chef!" Ethan exclaimed.

TWO

THE FAMOUS CHEF ARRIVES

"Who?" I exclaimed.

"Sebastian LeClair! The star of *Taste the Wrath*. Don't tell me you've never watched the show!"

"I guess I haven't." I shrugged. And after experiencing his rude behavior, I would *never* watch it. I bet Clara and Mystery did, though. "Why is a famous TV chef in Glenwood Springs?"

"You don't watch celebrity gossip shows either?" Ethan exclaimed, horrified at the thought.

"I don't."

"He retired out of the blue, quit the TV show, sold the Manhattan restaurant, and moved here. I've been hoping to run into him." He looked chagrined. "Oops. No offense."

"It's definitely not all it's cracked up to be," I assured him. "With that said, I'm off to the bakery," I declared, ensuring I had everything I'd dumped on the floor.

"Have fun!" Ethan called after me.

As I drove to Juliet's bakery, I struggled to shake the anger bubbling inside me. Sebastian LeClair, this so-called celebrity chef, knocked me on my backside and then dared to blame me for it. Seriously. I may have said a few inappropriate things in my lifetime, but I never knocked anyone down. The more I thought about his rude behavior, the more I wondered who this guy was and why he moved here. Why would you suddenly leave your fancy restaurant and TV show to retire and move to a quiet town like this? Don't get me wrong. This was the greatest place ever. But for someone like him? I couldn't imagine how our sleepy little mountain town would be enough.

I found a parking spot on Grand Street down the block from the bakery, and the moment I got out of the bus, I inhaled deeply; the heavenly scent of freshly baked cookies mingling with the spicy smell of cinnamon rolls filled my senses. It was like a comforting hug melting away some of my earlier frustration. Forget Mr. Fancy Pants SebastianLe-Clair. *My* friend had a bakery, and I was eager to taste some pie.

Sol Conceptions bright yellow awning stood out along a block filled with other cute shops calling to tourists and townspeople alike. The large bay window offered passersby a peek inside a world that smelled like fresh bread and sugar. The cheerful bell over the door announced my entrance into a place my waistline reminded me I enjoyed visiting far too often.

The walls inside were a soft, buttery yellow, meant to remind customers of sunlight on a fresh spring afternoon. Golden-yellow-topped counters showed off rows of pastries and cookies as if they were jewels on display, while the large glass showcase held everything from lemon tarts with their delicate, sunny filling to perfectly round cinnamon rolls. Behind the counter were shelves stacked with loaves of crusty bread, their flour-dusted tops adding a touch of rustic charm. Small tables scattered across the bakery, each holding an adorable vase with fresh purple mums.

Wendy was already seated at a table near the counter, with her latest crochet project - a tiny orange sweater, no doubt for one of her naked, excuse me, sphynx cats - dangling from her fingers. The first time I met her rescued cats, I shouted, "They're naked!" Which Wendy didn't find humorous at all. I still argued she could have at least warned me.

When the cats' original guardian passed away, the rescue desperately tried to find a home for three bonded cats. But after months passed with no offers in sight, they were prepared to split them up to get them adopted. After all, who would be willing to take on three cats at once? Turns out Wendy was wacky (and generous!) enough to do that. And she named them Rabbit, Eeyore, and Roo. When she insisted she would knit them sweaters for the cold winter, I was sure they'd never wear them. But they do. Most of the time, anyway.

Juliet, a sun witch, stood behind the counter, her shoulder-length blonde hair twisted into a braid with a dusting of flour on her bangs and a smudge of chocolate on her cheek. Today, she had replaced her turquoise-colored cat glasses with red ones. I liked to think of Juliet as the cautious mother of our group. She was always worried about us and frequently warned me not to act on impulse as I often did. Much to her chagrin!

Wendy paused her crochet project to give me one of her famous big hugs. My tattooed and pierced best friend, a potions witch, owned the Looking Glass Bookstore, my second favorite place after the bakery. (Although it was nearly a tie.) "Holly! Perfect timing. You look like you need a hug. What happened?"

"I just 'met' the famous Sebastian LeClair," I told them.

"You did?" Juliet exclaimed. "Hang on, why did you just use air quotes?"

"He knocked me on my rear at the pool and told me to watch where I was going!" I harumphed.

"Oh yeah, he's not exactly known for his pleasant demeanor," Wendy explained.

"The guy who works at the check-in counter said he moved here?"

"Yes! A real celebrity in our midst. It's so exciting!" Juliet insisted.

"You wouldn't call it exciting if you'd been the one to land on your rear," I complained, rubbing my backside for emphasis.

"Perhaps it was just a mistake?" Juliet offered.

"In that case, he could have said, 'Oh my gosh, I'm so sorry, let me help you,'" I pointed out with a steely-eyed stare.

"Well, anyway, are you ladies ready to eat some pumpkin pie?" she asked, brushing off my complaint, which I quickly forgot the moment she said pie.

"I'm famished!" Wendy insisted. Wendy was one of those annoying people who was always hungry and could eat anything. And often did!

Meanwhile, Juliet and I were more like regular people. Juliet was on the short side but cute and curvy. She was shaped like a baker you could trust. And I, well, I already explained my need for an annual pass at the Hot Springs.

Wendy put aside her crocheting while we pushed together two tables to make room for the tasting. We each sat on the opposite side, eagerly awaiting the pie.

Juliet disappeared into the back room of the bakery, reappearing several minutes later, carefully balancing a tray with two small plates labeled "A," which she placed in front of us.

"Dude, that's it?" Wendy asked. "It's like, two bites if that."

Juliet sighed and rolled her eyes. "This is the first one. It's why it's labeled A. There are two more to go."

"No," Wendy protested. "I mean, this is a tiny sample size."

"You can have the rest of the pie when we're done."

"Outstanding!" Wendy exclaimed.

I closed my eyes as I savored the first bite, then looked at Juliet with a grin and said, "If this doesn't win, I'll eat my pink bus - it tastes like autumn and cozy nights in front of the fire!" I laughed when I realized I sounded like Clara.

"Calm down," Juliet responded with a smile. "It's only the first one."

She turned to Wendy, who took a bite, her eyes widening as she chewed, "By all the whiskers on my hairless cats, girl, this is divine - it's like you baked all the comfort of fall straight into this pie."

"I'm glad you liked it, but don't just say that because you think it's what I want to hear. This is a serious competition. I've been trying to beat Mabel Winchester for three years, and I swear I'll do anything to win this year."

"Anything?" Wendy asked, her mouth still full of pie. But once she finished her sample, she speared the rest of mine, stuffing it in her mouth.

"*Anything!*" Juliet exclaimed right before she disappeared into the back for the second sample.

She returned with the same tray and two new plates of sample-sized pie pieces labeled B.

I took a bite of the second sample and paused, my brow furrowing slightly as I said, "This one's good, Jules, but there's something... different about it - like it's trying a bit too hard to be fancy, you know?"

"Okay. I'm not surprised you think that." She turned to Wendy again.

Wendy tilted her head thoughtfully as she tasted the second pie, then mused, "I want to say it's like this one is too prim and proper but no fun." After which she still stole the rest of my sample.

"I reckon it's a no on that one," Juliet said, her East Texas accent making an appearance before she disappeared into the back again for the final sample. After she brought out the next sample, I took a bite, and my mouth dropped open, which I promptly covered because I was still chewing. "This is the one. If you don't enter this one, I'll never speak to you again."

"Noted," Juliet said, looking slightly alarmed.

Wendy let her head drop back as she savored the last sample, then snapped it forward with a mischievous grin, declaring, "If this pie were one of my spells, it'd be the kind that makes everyone fall in love with me - it's absolutely bewitching, darling!" she shouted, throwing her arms in the air dramatically while attempting once again to reach for my sample. This time, I was ready and slapped her hand away.

"Ow!" she pouted, rubbing her hand.

"Don't steal my pie, don't get slapped."

"Well, butter my backside and call me a biscuit, that settles it. Option B," Juliet responded laughingly. "So, who wants a full slice?"

"Me!" Wendy said.

"Which one?" Juliet asked.

"All of them!"

"And you?" she said, looking at me.

"I'd like a small slice of option C, please." In reality, I wanted the entire pie, but that was Wendy's deal, not mine. While my stomach wanted the whole thing, my thighs reminded me a small slice was plenty.

"Could we get some espresso to go with that?" Wendy asked as Juliet disappeared into the back room for additional pie.

"I can make it!" I said, hopping up from my seat. As I tamped down the coffee grounds, I turned to face the ladies. "So, about this Sebastian LeClair character," I began as Juliet and Wendy perked up over the mention of the celebrity chef. "Don't you think it's weird that he suddenly moved to our little town?" I raised an eyebrow, my skepticism evident. "I mean, a big-shot TV chef with a wildly popular restaurant in Manhattan just throws it all away and moves to Glenwood Springs for retirement and a 'quiet life'? It doesn't add up."

"Ohhh, what if he's hiding something?" Wendy offered.

"Like what?" Juliet said.

Wendy leaned in conspiratorially, her eyes sparkling with excitement, while she whispered, "What if he's actually on the run from a secret underground culinary mafia? Maybe he stole a priceless secret recipe for the world's most addictive tiramisu, and now they're after him!"

"Do you ever think about anything other than food?" Juliet asked.

Wendy nodded vigorously. "Cats. I think about cats."

"When does the contest start?" I asked Juliet, shaking my head at our charismatic friend.

"The pies have to be delivered by 7 PM tonight, where they will be kept under lock and key in a special refrigerator in the kitchen at the Red Castle Hotel until the judging begins tomorrow. So, after we finish here, I'll bake a new version of pie C, " Juliet says, pointing to the now empty pie tin, prompting Wendy to shrug shamelessly.

"This has been great; thank you for the pie and conversation, ladies," I told them as I cleared away our plates to take into the back room, "but I have an appointment on 10th Street about a ghost."

"You guys!" Wendy exclaimed excitedly when her phone pinged with a news alert. "Breaking news: Celebrity chef Sebastian LeClair announced as surprise judge for tomorrow's Great Harvest Pie Showdown."

THREE

STIRRING THE POT

"Then it's a good thing it's you and not me in the contest," I pointed at Juliet. "Although he probably won't remember running into me."

"Sebastian LeClair is one of the judges?" Juliet exclaimed, her brow furrowed.

"What's wrong with that?" Wendy asked.

"Why would they throw in a newcomer at the last minute like that? The judges have always been just regular people from around town. You know, like a small business owner, or the president of the Chamber of Commerce, someone from the mayor's office. Those kinds of people."

"Is it bad that he's a judge?" I asked.

"Are you kidding me? Sebastian LeClair is a real chef! He trained at LeCordon Bleu! *And* he's a celebrity. He has a TV show. Dadgummit! I should start on a new recipe."

"No!" Wendy and I exclaimed.

"Honey, just stick with Option C," Wendy said. "Holly and I thought it was out of this world and LeClair will too. You'll see. You don't need to impress some snooty ol' chef anyway. The whole town knows you're incredible."

"Oh dear, oh dear, oh dear," Juliet muttered, shaking her head, wandering to the back room again.

"I'll deal with her," Wendy assured me. "You go to work."

"Do whatever you can to convince her not to start over."

"I will," Wendy said with a wink.

I PULLED UP TO MYRTLE HIGGINS' house on 10th Street, pausing to study it. Like certain homes in Glenwood Springs, it was (what I assumed anyway) impressive back in the day. Like something you'd see in a storybook. Climbing roses and ivy growing up trellises, while a wrap-around porch, with a swing and pots overflowing with colorful wild-flowers, were a perfect place to pause and enjoy a glass of iced tea and conversation. The picturesque front yard boasted a whimsical collection of garden gnomes peeking from behind an ancient oak tree.

Mrs. Higgins had regularly complained to the authorities that the knick-knacks in her home were moved when she wasn't looking, and the furniture was rearranged when she knew she hadn't done it. Her adult son threatened to put her in a nursing home because he was convinced she was losing her mind. But Mrs. Higgins just knew someone was breaking into her home in the middle of the night to move things.

She had called the sheriff's office so many times that Sheriff Mack finally contacted me about it. Me! I was stunned, to say the least, that he actually requested my help, considering how often he complained about my interfering in investigations. Would wonders never cease? While I certainly considered poor Mrs. Higgins might be suffering from dementia, there was also a good chance that she had a ghost friend and didn't realize it.

"Who is it?" I heard a feeble voice call from behind the doorway after I rang the doorbell.

"It's me, Mrs. Higgins, Holly Daniel. I'm the Paranormal Private Investigator sent from the Sheriff's Office."

I listened while she undid several locks on the front door. This poor woman. She must be terrified, thinking that someone was breaking in every night.

She opened the door, appraising me carefully. Myrtle Higgins was a petite, silver-haired woman with bright, sparkling blue eyes. Her floral housedress, the glasses she wore around her neck with a silver chain, and fuzzy pink slippers gave her the appearance of a gentle soul - until she opened her mouth and let loose a stream of colorful language that would make a sailor blush.

"Oh my!" I exclaimed after hearing her thoughts on this mysterious person breaking into her house every night. Sheriff Mack expected me to deliver a written report on my findings. I didn't even know how to spell some of the words she used!

"Miss Daniel, I tell you, some no good, dirty, rotten thief has been breaking in here at night and messing with my things!" she exclaimed, her hands trembling as she threw them in the air. "Every morning, I wake up, and my knick-knacks are all catawampus!"

I stepped toward her, my voice gentle but firm. "Mrs. Higgins, I believe you. Can you tell me more about what's been moved?"

After meeting her, I didn't think for a moment that she had dementia. Nor did I think someone was breaking into her house at night for the sheer pleasure of rearranging her things. It was clearly the work of a spirit, and if we talked long enough, it should appear. It could be a poltergeist that moved from place to place or a ghost who lived on the premises and could move solid objects. Some spirits were adept at manipulating physical objects, while others couldn't push so much as a feather. Much of it was still a mystery to me.

Myrtle's eyes darted around the room, recalling what had been moved. "It's those little porcelain figures my late Herbert got me. Used to face the window, now they're all turned around like they're watchin' me. And my chairs! They're always pushed in when I go to bed, but come mornin', they're pulled out like someone's been sittin' in 'em."

"I see," I nodded, jotting notes, stalling for time. Sometimes, the ghosts appeared right away when they knew someone nearby could see them. Other times, they played coy and waited until they thought it was safe. "And your son thinks..."

"That old fool thinks his mama's gone round the bend!" Myrtle interrupted, her voice rising. "He wants to ship me off to one of those boring retirement villages in Florida. More like a retirement prison if you ask me."

I couldn't help but smile at her spunk. "Well, Mrs. Higgins, I don't think you're losing your mind. In fact, I have a strong suspicion about what is happening here."

"Ha! I was right!" she leaned in, her eyes wide. "You think someone is breaking into my home too, don't you."

"No, Sheriff Mack called me because he suspects you have a ghost, and I'm here to confirm it."

"A ghost! Well, now you're the one who's soundin' nutty!" Myrtle exclaimed.

"I promise you, I'm not nutty. I see dead people."

Myrtle laughed uproariously. "Maybe you're the one who needs to move to a retirement village."

"I know, it sounds crazy. And many people have thought that about me. Do you know that I've been able to talk to ghosts ever since I was a kid, but my parents assumed it was imaginary friends? Then, one day, my friend's grandmother died, and we went to her house with a casserole to pay our respects." Myrtle leaned in closer, wondering what I would say next. I hoped the ghost would appear soon. I really didn't want to be here for hours waiting for whoever it was.

"They sent the kids to the backyard to play on the swing set, and Grandma's ghost appeared to me."

"Get out!" Myrtle exclaimed.

"I promise you, she did. She told me she'd hidden money in the attic and wanted her family to have it."

"What did you do next?"

"I went inside and told the adults."

"Did they believe you?" she asked, putting on her glasses and leaning even closer.

"Of course not. But I was so insistent someone finally went to check."

"Was it there? Was the money there?"

"It sure was!" I said proudly.

"Did you tell them grandma's ghost told you?" she asked, removing her glasses and rubbing them with a lace hanky tucked in her sleeve.

"I did." I nodded. "But they were convinced I must have overheard Grandma talking about it before she passed, and that's how I knew. But that's when my parents finally realized that all my imaginary friends and knowing about the money was me seeing ghosts."

"Do your parents live in Glenwood Springs, dear?"

"No," I sighed. "They passed away when I was very

young. After that, I was raised in several foster homes, and, well, here I am. Helping you with what I'm sure is a ghost."

"That is fascinating. Although I'm still not convinced, I have a ghost here."

"I am," I said firmly when a spirit dressed as a butler walked into the room.

"Good afternoon, sir," I said to him.

"Well, I'll be," he chuckled. "You're real."

"And so are you."

Myrtle's eyes grew round as saucers. "Are you seriously trying to tell me you're talking to a ghost right now?"

"I am."

"Prove it."

"Can you tell me something that only Myrtle would know?" I asked him. "And don't..." I cut him off before he could say something too personal, "make it weird. If you know what I mean."

"Very well, madam," the ghost said. "Mrs. Higgins prepares a cup of tea with a special tea cup every afternoon at precisely 2:00. She never misses a day, and she whistles 'What a Wonderful World' because that was her husband's favorite song."

When I repeated it to her, she stared in shock. "Well, I'll be..." she let out another string of words that I can't say in public. "Ask him why he's moving my stuff!"

"I'm simply tidying up as I did when I was alive," he responded.

"He says he's tidying up," I repeated. I practically saw a light bulb go on over her head when she finally figured it out.

"That's why the dust rag and the can of Pledge keep moving!"

The ghost butler nodded. "Edgar Pemberton at your

service. You see, once upon a time, this home belonged to the grand estate of the Worthington family, a wealthy family in Glenwood Springs. I served them faithfully for many years. However, one fateful winter evening, while preparing the house for the Worthington's' annual Christmas soiree, I suffered a heart attack at the foot of the staircase. As I felt my life force slipping away, all I could think about was that the silver still needed polishing. The house has changed hands many times since then, and unfortunately, its grandeur slowly faded. But as Mrs. Higgins grew older," he continued, pointing at her, "I noticed how she struggled with the upkeep of the old house. So I decided to help out."

I repeated his story to Myrtle but added, "I can tell him to stop if you want," I offered while secretly thinking I wouldn't mind having a ghost butler clean *my* house while I slept.

"No!" she exclaimed. "I think Mr. Pemberton and I will get along just fine. Would it be okay to tell him where I want him to put my things?" she asked while he nodded happily.

I left with a small box of homemade cookies and a smile on my face. The jobs I took on weren't always this easy or this pleasant. The ghost who was eaten by a shark and spit back out on the beach still made me shudder every time I thought about it.

When my stomach growled, I remembered that aside from the bowl of Cheerios I had for breakfast, all I'd eaten today was a bit of pumpkin pie. If I planned to keep going, I had to stop for lunch.

I pulled into the parking lot of the Glenwood Grinders Sandwich Shop, thinking that a club sandwich with extra tomatoes on sourdough would be just the thing to get me through the rest of the day.

It was a beloved local institution that had served sandwiches for three generations. It was known for its cozy atmosphere and signature, mouthwatering Mile-High Pastrami on Rye. The line often stretched out the door, but nobody minded the wait. It was all part of the experience. Thankfully, the line was shorter today, and as I pulled open the glass door, I relished the scent of freshly baked bread mingled with savory notes of roasting meats and the sharp tang of pickles and mustard. I was so busy daydreaming about my sandwich it took me a moment to realize the usual buzz of lunchtime chatter was strangely non-existent.

Yet, I quickly discovered why when a familiar angry voice echoed across the small space. It belonged to Sebastian LeClair, whose face was red with fury as he berated a young waitress on the verge of tears. The poor girl, barely out of her teens, clutched her order pad like a shield while LeClair launched a tirade about the "abysmal quality" of his Reuben sandwich.

The other patrons, a mix of locals and tourists, sat frozen in their booths while those still in line at the counter inched away from the bellowing LeClair. Sandwiches sat forgotten as the spectacle unfolded. Some customers were shocked, others embarrassed, and a few seemed almost gleeful at the drama while they recorded the dustup on their phones, no doubt already composing social media posts in their heads. Joe, the owner, stood frozen behind the counter, his usual jovial expression replaced by a look of concern and growing anger.

As a kid raised in foster care with hand-me-down clothes and a battered lunch box that squeaked when I opened it, I was often the victim of ignorant bullies, and it infuriated me when someone like Sebastian used his size and reputation to bully others. I didn't care how big he was, and I didn't care that I was supposed to be controlling my temper. Someone had to stop this. I stepped forward to tell him exactly what I thought he should do with his Reuben sandwich when Sheriff Mack and two deputies appeared in the doorway.

FOUR

A DEADLY SLICE

Sheriff Mack's annoyed expression made it clear that he had come here for lunch and not to handle the out-of-control Sebastian LeClair. But when he realized what was happening, a sharp nod at his deputies sent them straight for LeClair while the customers returned to eating their lunches when they realized the show was over.

"Ms. Daniel," he greeted me with a brief nod.

"Sheriff Mack."

"I just got a call from Mrs. Higgins."

I smiled, knowing I'd done well. "I'm sure you did."

"She said you're a lifesaver and could never thank you enough."

"I'm just happy to help," I responded proudly.

"So it really was a ghost?"

I nodded vigorously. "It was. A butler ghost who was cleaning her house."

"Glad to hear it," he said. "That's one less residence we'll have to visit on a regular basis."

"You'll get my invoice by the end of the day," I assured him.

"Have you ordered yet?" he asked.

"No, I just walked in to find our new neighbor, Sebastian LeClair, over there chewing out the waitress."

"I've heard rumors. That guy sounds like a piece of work," he muttered.

"I met him when he knocked me down at the pool this morning."

"He what?" Sheriff Mack exclaimed, looking angry.

Sheriff Mack, or Surly Steve as Wendy, Juliet, and I liked to call him behind his back, was a tall, handsome man with short dark hair and pretty eyes. (Although I was sure he wouldn't appreciate being described like that!) Wendy and Juliet were convinced we had a thing for each other even though I kept telling them they were out of their minds. Clara thought Sheriff Mack was simply divine. Mystery didn't appreciate it when he came to the house, which was weird. Given her issues with authority figures, I was secretly convinced she was a fugitive in one of her previous nine lives.

"It's okay. I mean, kind of. I wasn't watching where I was going, and we ran into each other, and I fell. But he was rude about it. I heard he moved here for a so-called retirement."

"That's what I heard too. But why did you say it like that? You sound skeptical."

"It doesn't add up. Fancy celebrity chef with a Michelin star restaurant quits without warning? It's almost more like he's hiding from something or someone," I suggested.

"I think you've been watching too many of Clara's True Crime documentaries," Sheriff Mack replied.

"C'mon, it doesn't sound even a bit suspicious to you?" I pressed.

"I have plenty of *real* crimes to keep me occupied. I don't need to go looking for them."

"Okay," I told him. "But when he turns out to be some sort of hoodlum, you can say I was right all along."

"I'll be sure to do that," he responded with what I was convinced was just a hint of a smile on his face, probably wanting to laugh over my use of the word hoodlum.

"You're next," he pointed out when the person in front of me left the order window.

"Hi. Yes, I'd like a club sandwich with extra tomato, fries, and an iced tea, please."

After I finished my order, I turned back to say something more to the sheriff, but he was talking to his deputies, who were nodding and gesturing to a calmer Sebastian LeClair.

That's how our conversations often ended. Abruptly. Sheriff Mack was a man of few words. Oh well, I had a lot more work to do before I called it a day. A few minutes later, I collected my order and headed out the door, still wondering why LeClair had really come to Glenwood.

THE FOLLOWING MORNING, I texted Juliet.

> Me: Did you deliver your pie?

> Juliet: I sure did! It's now safe and sound in the Red Castle Hotel kitchen.

> Me: Why all the security? It's not exactly a high-stakes competition.

Juliet: I think they do it to make us feel important. But I also heard it's to prevent cheating.

Me: Cheating? Who would cheat?

Juliet: Rumor has it that Mabel, another one of the contestants, cheats.

Me: Seriously?

Juliet: Yep!

Me: Please tell me you used the third recipe that Wendy and I liked so much.

Juliet: Yes! I hope the judges (especially Sebastian!) approve of it.

Me: I'm sure they'll love it.

Juliet: Don't forget, the competition starts at 2:00.

Me: I'll be there!

THE RED CASTLE Hotel hosted the Great Harvest Pie Showdown baking contest every fall in their ballroom. The opulent hotel was built in the late 1800s as a luxury resort for the wealthy. Developers bet on the hot springs draw and built a hotel to go with it. Several ghosts have told me stories about famous people who have visited in the past, including Theodore Roosevelt, William Taft, and Molly Brown.

A spirit-maid named Ethel swore to me that she made a stuffed bear from fabric scraps for President Roosevelt while he was visiting, and that's how the teddy bear was invented. I wasn't sure I believed her, but it was an interesting story, that's for sure.

They used it as a naval convalescent hospital during World War II, with a prison and a morgue in the basement. Which, as you can imagine, only added to its mystique. Tourists and staff have reported numerous spirit sightings for decades, including faces in windows, voices, perfume and cigar scents, and even typewriter noises. As a Spirit Communicator, I could assure them these things were real. If they ever asked, of course.

The building was a symbol of turn-of-the-century grandeur. The ghosts told me the architecture was styled after the Italian Renaissance because the architect thought it stood out against the rugged mountains surrounding it.

Some said its most striking feature was the central tower, rising several stories above the main structure and crowned with a steep, pitched roof. Flanking the central tower were two wings stretching out on either side, framing a garden courtyard as a hidden oasis, with a tiered marble fountain as the centerpiece.

Stone pathways wound through meticulously maintained flower beds, where late-blooming mums in rich burgundies and golds added vibrant splashes of color. Wrought iron tables and benches, painted a glossy black and adorned with scrollwork details, were strategically placed throughout the garden, offering guests peaceful nooks to enjoy their morning coffee or afternoon tea while taking in the spectacular mountain views that loomed beyond the hotel's red brick walls.

When I moved to Glenwood, I got a bartending job at

the hotel and, much to my chagrin, was immediately pulled into solving a ghost-related mystery. But that job kickstarted my career as a Paranormal Private Investigator. And I still occasionally filled in as a bartender when they were short-handed.

The hotel manager, Gabriel Molina, was at a conference in Washington DC at the moment. Juliet and Wendy often claimed he had a thing for me, too. Just because I was a widow, every man who was even somewhat close to my age was somehow fair game for them to try and set me up. They were my age. Why didn't they date one of these eligible bachelors if they were so great?

My late husband was one of the few people in my lifetime who knew that I was an actual Spirit Communicator. He was also the first real family I had after my parents died. So when he died too... Well. Let's just say I wasn't keen on getting into another relationship.

Following directional arrows to the ballroom, I greeted several ghosts and guests as we streamed through the lobby. Colorful banners and balloons announced the annual competition, complete with posters heralding the addition of the famous TV chef Sebastian LeClair. I was surprised to see news crews on the scene as well! So much for LeClair living the quiet life.

The grand ballroom of the Red Castle Hotel featured soaring coffered ceilings adorned with crystal chandeliers that cast a warm, golden glow across the polished hardwood floor below. Ornate crown molding traced the room's perimeter, its intricate designs complementing the floor-to-ceiling windows that lined the far wall, their heavy velvet drapes pulled back to reveal stunning views of the mountains beyond.

At one end of the ballroom was a long table that

included the three original judges: Marlowe Blackwood, a retiring state legislator for our district; Rosemary Tate, the owner of a popular bicycle shop on 6th Street; and Wes Holbrook, a river rafting tour guide. Then, there was Sebastian LeClair at the far end, indicating that he was somehow separate from the others. Was that his choice or the hotel's? Each judge had a placard in front of them with their name, but LeClair's included the title *Head Judge*. It was hard not to sigh dramatically at the celebrity treatment. And was it just me, or were the other judges throwing him sidelong glances, annoyed by this newcomer's sudden celebrity status?

On either side of the judges' table were individual stations where the contestants sat. I spotted Juliet right away, but when I waved, she looked right through me. She was wringing her hands nervously and repeatedly adjusting her glasses.

I wondered how I'd ever find a seat in this crowd when I saw Wendy waving at me and pointing to an empty seat beside her. Just as I sat down, the announcer urged everyone to take their seats so the judging could begin. A moment later, the hotel wait staff brought in each pie, placing it in front of the contestant, who would then, one by one, present their pie to the Head Chef to start the inspection and tasting. They would be judged on scent, presentation, attractiveness, and, of course, taste and texture. The atmosphere was charged with excitement and nervous energy while the ushers continued to urge the guests to take their seats.

While we waited for the judging to start, Wendy pointed out each of the contestants:

"The woman next to Juliet," she whispered, "is Mabel Winchester. She's a spell witch who has won the contest

three years in a row," she paused while looking conspirator-
ial, "rumor has it, she cheated."

"Juliet told me that too," I whispered back.

Mabel was a stout woman with iron-gray hair pulled
back into a severe bun. She was fussing with her pie while
appearing to mutter into it. I wasn't sure if she was talking to
herself or whispering a spell. She owned a shop in town
called: Mabel's Magical Preserves. While the rules stated no
witchcraft was allowed, it was commonly understood that
many witches added a little extra something to their
creations. But an adjustment like a love potion or truth
serum was strictly forbidden and could get a contestant
disqualified.

"Next to her is Eliot Thornfield," Wendy continued.
Eliot was a tall, wiry man with a crooked grin and eyes that
seemed to catch the light in a peculiar way. He appeared
eager for the competition to start as he squirmed in his seat
and repeatedly fussed with the long sleeves of his shirt. I was
sure I remembered seeing him in the bar last week, because I
noticed he walked with a limp. "He's a best-selling author
who's new to the area," Wendy said. "He's supposed to be
here writing a book on the history of Glenwood Springs."

"You don't believe it?"

She shrugged. "For a best-selling author, no one seems
to have heard of him."

"Next to him is Daisy Thompson," Wendy continued.
Daisy was a young woman who was clearly far more
nervous than Juliet. She wore thick glasses and kept biting
her fingernails. An anxious woman, who Wendy said was
Daisy's mother, hovered nearby. "Mom owns a barbeque
restaurant and constantly pressures Daisy to follow in her
footsteps." While Daisy appeared to be urging her mother to

sit down, she refused until one of the ushers insisted Mom take a seat in the audience.

"The guy who looks like he has professionally styled hair and makeup is Reverend Gregory Fletchen, or Pastor Greg as the locals call him," Wendy explained. At first glance, Pastor Greg looked relatively young, but when I watched him further, I decided he must be about the same age as Sebastian LeClair, only with more makeup and perhaps some cosmetic work. I had seen him around town and noticed his sandy hair always appeared windswept. If I had to pick a fictional character to describe him, I'd say he reminded me of Professor Lockhart in the *Harry Potter* series.

The premise behind the annual competition was to foster community spirit and celebrate the fall season. Wendy explained they liked to include a mix of professional bakers like Juliet, and community members like Pastor Greg, and sometimes they added a newcomer with an interesting occupation like Eliot.

The host of the competition was Vern Cartwright, Glenwood's mayor. He was a jovial man with a bushy mustache and a booming voice, and when he stepped up to the microphone, the crowd quieted. "Ladies and gentlemen," he called out, his voice overriding the remaining chatter, "please take your seats. The moment we've all been waiting for is about to begin!"

As the crowd settled, he continued, "Welcome to the 75th annual Great Harvest Pie Showdown, a beloved tradition that has brought our community together since 1948. Today, we celebrate not just the finest pies in Glenwood Springs but the spirit of friendly competition and the rich tapestry of flavors that make our town so special. Please note that there is a program change, and Juliet Beaumont of Sol Conceptions Bakery will go first."

The crowd murmured, while Juliet appeared shocked and ill at the same time. If it were me, I think I'd be happy to go first and get it over with. But what prompted the change? First, they added LeClair as a judge, and now they were changing the order of the pie tasting. So many last-minute changes, and what if they were all at LeClair's insistence? I had to admit, I wasn't a fan of Glenwood's newcomer. I didn't care how famous he was.

The mayor paused, letting his gaze sweep across the room. "And let's not forget, folks, once our esteemed judges have made their decisions and awarded the coveted Golden Rolling Pin, we'll kick off our harvest celebration right here in this very ballroom. So, get those taste buds ready, and may the best pie win!"

With a flourish, he gestured to the judges' table, where Sebastian LeClair and his fellow judges sat, forks at the ready. The room held its collective breath as Juliet stood up, smoothed her apron, cleared her throat, and walked over to where LeClair was seated. When she placed her pie in front of him, the crowd applauded softly, almost as if they were watching a professional golfer sink a putt at a PGA Championship.

Sebastian LeClair leaned over Juliet's pumpkin pie, his nose nearly touching what I considered a perfect crust. He inhaled deeply, then straightened up with a theatrical flourish. "Ah," he proclaimed, his affected French accent thick and pompous, "une tarte à la citrouille classique. You know, during my time at Le Cordon Bleu in Paris, I once created a pumpkin soufflé that brought tears to the eyes of a three-star Michelin chef."

He paused, waiting for impressed murmurs from the crowd. "Of course, that was after I had perfected my technique under the tutelage of Master Patissier Pierre Hermé himself." Sebastian ran his finger along the edge of the pie dish, inspecting it closely. "I remember an autumn in Provence, where I sourced the most exquisite poti marron squash for my award-winning 'Harvest Moon Galette.' It caused quite the stir in the culinary world, you know."

He finally picked up his famous golden fork, a piece of gold-plated cutlery he was well known for using to taste dishes on his show. (Yes, I searched for him online after learning he'd moved here.) He appeared poised to take a bite but added, "Let's see if this humble offering can live up to such lofty standards, shall we?" The crowd watched in tense silence as Sebastian, with all the gravitas of a king, finally tasted Juliet's pie. For a moment, I was worried that Juliet might pass out from nerves.

"By the way," he started as he chewed, "you may not know this, but I have honed my sense of smell and taste to detect when artificial ingredients are used in baking..."

What the heck was he blathering about? And why wouldn't he stop talking? Juliet's face went from nervous to enraged.

Sebastian LeClair's eyes widened as he stopped talking and swallowed his first bite of the pie, his face contorting into an expression of surprise and discomfort. He opened his mouth as if to speak but instead let out a strangled gasp, his hand flying to his throat as he struggled to breathe. The crowd watched in horrified silence as the famous chef's eyes rolled back in his head, and he crumpled to the floor with a sickening thud, his body convulsing briefly before going terrifyingly still.

The mayor ran to LeClair's side and reached for his neck.

"He's dead!" he cried.

FIVE

THE LAST JUDGMENT

For a heart-stopping moment, the ballroom sat silent. The disbelief was thick and suffocating. LeClair's lifeless form sprawled grotesquely on the polished floor, his once-piercing eyes now dull and vacant, stared unseeingly at the stunned onlookers, while his meticulously styled hair was matted with pumpkin pie filling, cinnamon, and whipped cream.

In a flash, like a broken spell, chaos erupted. Screams, gasps, and panicked shouts echoed throughout the room as people leaped to their feet, their chairs screeching against the floor, while everyone stumbled about in horror. Some were desperate to leave in a hurry, while others wanted a closer look at the famous chef, now lying dead on the floor. Juliet's face drained of color, her eyes wide with disbelief as she stared at her pie - the very one LeClair had just tasted.His golden fork lay unattended on the floor until one of the audience members who scrambled to leave, accidentally kicked it, sending it clattering across the space.

The other judges stood gawking, their faces masked with shock and fear. Someone shouted for a doctor, while several others frantically dialed 911, their voices shrill with panic, relaying what they just witnessed.

The assistant hotel manager, Gerald, a tall, thin man with a receding hairline, suddenly appeared at the front of the room, attempting to calm the chaos. "Ladies and gentlemen, please remain calm!" he shouted, his arms raised placatingly. "I know this is a shocking turn of events, but I must ask everyone to stay seated until the authorities arrive - your cooperation is crucial at this time."

"Authorities!" a young woman in the front row exclaimed. "Why should we wait for the authorities?"

Good point. He must have had a heart attack, considering he wasn't the healthiest-looking guy in the world, after all. He was a large man who, if I were blunt, I'd say the last time he exercised was around sixth grade gym class. I couldn't blame him, though. If I were a chef, it would be nearly impossible to keep me from eating my weight in all that delicious food.

"Just do what the man says!" someone shouted from across the room. "We'll be out of here soon."

Several minutes ticked by, but as the initial shock wore off, it was replaced by a growing restlessness rippling through the crowd. "This is ridiculous," a portly man in a plaid shirt growled, his face red with indignation, "I didn't sign up to be a witness to someone's death - I'm leaving!" His words galvanized the others, and a chorus of agreement rose from various corners of the room, with several people edging towards the exits despite Gerald's increasingly desperate pleas for order.

Juliet stood frozen behind her station, her face ashen and her hands trembling uncontrollably. Her eyes, wide with disbelief and horror, kept darting between Sebastian LeClair's lifeless form and her pumpkin pie, as if she couldn't quite comprehend what happened. I didn't think any of us could comprehend this.

"We have to help Juliet!" Wendy insisted, thankfully wiping any more macabre thoughts from my head. She was right. Our friend needed us.

As Wendy and I moved toward Juliet, and a large group of people moved toward the door, despite Gerald's insistence they stay put, Sheriff Mack, accompanied by a deputy, marched into the room, bellowing at everyone to stop. While Gerald couldn't quell the crowd, Surly Steve sure could.

On Sheriff Mack's heels were paramedics and the Garfield County Coroner's Office. How did a fun and light-hearted experience suddenly become such a somber scene?

Sheriff Mack leaned over, whispering something to his deputy, who then announced that he needed all the contestants and the remaining judges to follow him immediately. Wendy and I shrugged apologetically at Juliet as she was escorted along with the others from the room. They were taking this awfully seriously for a heart attack, weren't they? Soon, the sheriff was joined by additional deputies while one of them guarded the pies.

"What's going on here?" I whispered to Wendy.

"Publicity," she said, tilting her head toward the TV cameras.

Oh. Yeah. I hadn't thought of that. This would obviously play on network news across the country tonight, and the authorities wanted to be seen taking it seriously.

"Everyone else, please take your seats immediately, and we'll get this processed as quickly as possible," Gerald called out.

Some of us groaned in complaint, hesitating momentarily as if we were prepared to defy the sheriff, but one withering look from the deputy stationed at the door and everyone quickly sat down.

"This is so weird," Wendy whispered while I nodded in agreement.

I waved Gerald over. "Isn't this a lot of official police business for a heart attack?"

Gerald shrugged. "I overheard one of the deputies saying that having a famous chef drop dead at a pie-tasting competition would bring a ton of unwanted publicity here, and they don't want to take even the smallest chance that it could be something else."

"Something else?" I asked while he shrugged again, hurrying away when Sheriff Mack called for him.

"I can't believe that happened after tasting Juliet's pie. She must be devastated," Wendy said.

"And she wasn't even supposed to go first!" I reminded her.

"That's right, why did they change the tasting order? Who was *supposed* to go first?"

"Beats me, and remember, LeClair wasn't even supposed to be a judge! If they hadn't thrown him in at the last minute, he could have just died of a heart attack eating breakfast at a diner, and poor Juliet wouldn't be so trau-matized."

Wendy gasped in horror. "I didn't even think of that!"

The deputies quickly made their way through the crowd. I wasn't sure what the audience could tell them anyway. That they all witnessed the same thing - a man dying from a heart attack? Not much to tell.

I wondered what kinds of questions they were asking Juliet right now. I felt horrible for her. She had the biggest heart of anyone I knew, and she would undoubtedly blame herself. I watched the paramedics pack up their gear and leave since they obviously weren't needed while I feared this could be bad publicity for Juliet. And as much as I tried not to stare, I noticed the coroner was wrapping up his work as well, while his assistants hefted LeClair's body onto the gurney. And no, before you ask, there was no sign of LeClair's ghost.

Just when I thought we'd never be excused, one of the deputies waved me over to talk. He asked what I had witnessed, and after I told him, he excused me. I wanted to go back and sit with Wendy, but he insisted I leave through a side door instead. Thankfully, within only a few minutes, Wendy joined me.

"I'm glad that's over!" she exclaimed. "This whole thing went south quickly, didn't it?"

"Yeah, what a shame. Of course, I'm upset the guy died, but I'm even more upset about Juliet. She has to be so freaked out, to say the least."

"You know she'll blame herself," Wendy pointed out. "And what do we do now? We should wait for her, right? But I'm starving," she complained, clutching at her stomach.

"Of course you are. They'll never let us back in the hotel, though. Not with all the police activity."

"What could be taking so long?" Wendy complained further. "And what do you think they're asking her? What I wouldn't give to be a fly on that wall."

"Ohhh!" I grabbed Wendy's elbow in excitement. "I have one better."

Her eyes widened in recognition. "A ghost!"

Even though they had a sheriff's deputy stationed at the front door, I took a chance and showed him my employee ID. Fortunately, it worked, and he waved us in. "Can you believe this is all because LeClair is a celebrity?" I shook my head. "Let's grab lunch at the bar while we wait."

The Red Castle Hotel Restaurant and Bar was lined with rich, dark wood paneling, giving the space a cozy, intimate feel. The bar was a magnificent piece of craftsmanship - a long, polished mahogany counter with intricate carvings along its edge, topped with a smooth, gleaming surface, while a grand stone fireplace dominated the southeast corner of the room. Today, it was unlit, but on a snowy winter day, its crackling flames warmed the room with comfortable leather armchairs and small tables clustered around it, offering guests a cozy spot for drinks and conversation.

Wendy and I settled into the high-backed cocoa-brown leather barstools at the counter when Jenny, the bartender, approached us.

"How did you ladies get in here?" she asked. "It's been dead - oops, I guess I shouldn't say that - with all the cops around. Were you at the competition?" She nodded when I waved my employee ID. "Ahhh, good thinking!"

"Could we get lunch, please?" Wendy begged.

"You'll have to excuse my friend here," I said. "She hasn't eaten in an entire hour."

"Sure," Jenny said laughingly, "what'll it be, hon?"

"I'll start with some onion rings," Wendy began, appraising the menu as if she hadn't already memorized it - she's in here so often when I work. "I'll follow that up with a cobb salad and throw in the Cuban sandwich with extra pickles."

Jenny's eyes widened. "Are you splitting that?" she asked, waving her pencil between us.

"No!" Wendy exclaimed.

"I'll go with a Caesar salad, please," I told her.

"Oh! And I'll finish with the peach biscuit cobbler!" Wendy exclaimed.

"I'll be right back!" Jenny said before heading to the kitchen.

"Where are all your ghost friends?" Wendy asked. "I need to know what's going on with Juliet!"

No sooner did she say that when Heidi, a young woman who passed in the 1970s after choking on an olive in her martini, appeared. "Hey there," she said, sitting on the counter next to us.

"Hey, I was hoping you'd show."

"Where you been, girl?" she asked.

"Just working, you know. So what's the gossip on the authorities questioning the judges and the contestants?"

"You want to know about your friend Juliet?"

"I do." I nodded.

"I was just in a room where they were questioning her."

"They have them in separate rooms?" I asked with surprise, while Heidi nodded.

"That can't be good," I told Wendy.

"What can't be good? You always do this. You forget I can only hear *your* responses."

"Sorry about that. Heidi tells me the contestants are all being questioned in separate rooms."

"Okay, you're right, that isn't good."

"That's not even the worst of it," Heidi said.

"Uh oh. What's the worst of it?" I cringed.

"I overheard the coroner talking to Sheriff Mack right before he left, and he thinks that Sebastian LeClair was poisoned."

SIX

BREAKING NEWS

"Poison!" I exclaimed.

"Poison!" Wendy echoed so loudly that people in the bar turned to stare. "Why did you say poison?" she hissed at me.

"Heidi overheard the Coroner's Office tell Sheriff Mack they think LeClair was poisoned," I whispered back.

"How is that even possible? I mean, how could they know it that fast?"

"I have no clue, but if it was poison, Juliet's was the only one he ate," I gulped. This was so bad.

"Look!" Wendy whispered again, tapping on my hand.

A shaken man stumbled into the bar, sitting two chairs away and ordering a beer.

"That's the pastor who was in the competition," Wendy reminded me.

"He doesn't look so good," I pointed out.

Pastor Greg chugged his beer before he caught Wendy and me staring at him. "It's been a tough day, okay? I don't normally do this," he explained.

"You're one of the pie competition contestants, aren't you?" I asked.

He nodded grimly. "I was. Great idea that turned out to be, huh?"

"What did the authorities ask you?" Wendy pressed. "What kinds of questions?"

"It was so weird. They asked a ton of questions about what I put in my pie, where I got the ingredients, and where I baked it. Did I bake the pie in the same place where I assembled the ingredients? What was in the pie crust? Did I really make it from scratch? Why would you ask questions like that unless you thought something was wrong?"

"They asked me the same questions," Eliot Thornfield said as he gingerly sat on the opposite side of Pastor Greg. "Do they know something we don't know?"

Given what Heidi told us and Pastor Greg and Eliot confirming an unusual line of questioning, I was very uneasy about this. But before I had a chance to discuss it further with Wendy, a pale and terrified Juliet approached us.

"Girl, what did they do to you?" Wendy cried, rushing to pull out a chair for our friend.

"Here, sit down," I told her, patting on the chair. "Can we get some water here, please?" I asked Jenny. "Are you okay? Do you want lunch? We can get you a sandwich."

"No thanks. I'm not hungry," Juliet mumbled.

"What happened? What did they ask you about?" Wendy pressed.

"Why are you asking me like that? It's not like I killed him!" Juliet responded, her bottom lip trembling.

"Of course not, honey; he obviously had a heart attack or stroke or something. Let's face it, I don't think he was the healthiest guy in the world," Wendy pointed out.

"Then why did they keep asking me where I got my ingredients, and did I invent the recipe myself, was the pie cooked at my bakery or at home and on and on and on. What is happening?" she moaned, dropping her head into her hands.

"They asked the pastor and Eliot the same questions," I said, hoping to make her feel better.

"But my pie was the only one he tasted!" she cried.

"I'm sure it was nothing but a coincidence," Wendy assured her.

"They told me not to leave town!" she continued.

"Here's the thing," Wendy said. "They'll take the body to the coroner's office, run a bunch of tests, discover it was a heart attack, and that's the last we'll hear about it. And you can put this crazy mess behind you."

"I hope so. I feel horrible he died like that, but I'll be relieved when they confirm it was natural causes. Am I a bad person if I'm worried about how this will affect my bakery? And what if they arrest me?"

"Whoa. Slow down there. Why would this affect your bakery?" I asked, not revealing I was already worried about it. "You have the most popular bakery in town. Heck, it's the most popular bakery anywhere. People drive all the way from Grand Junction and Vail for your cakes alone. Just because some famous chef died tasting your pie doesn't mean your business will suffer."

"But I'm telling you, my pie was the only one he tasted. What if that gets around?"

"I'm sure no one will even notice, and it won't last long if they do. It will last until the next interesting news story comes up. Worst case scenario you'll have a big sale or something. Give everyone another reason to visit," I insisted, yet it felt forced even as I said it. I was increasingly worried about her.

"I hope you're right," Juliet sniffled. "I still can't believe this happened."

"Look, there's another contestant," I pointed out right before Mabel also sat at the bar. The bar ended up being a popular place today. "I bet they asked her the same questions as you, the pastor, and Eliot. In fact, I'll go check," I insisted, pushing my chair back and marching over to where Mabel was seated.

"Hi there, excuse me, Ms. Winchester. How's it going?"

"I've had better days!" she bellowed. "Barkeep! Tequila shot!!"

I bet Sebastian LeClair never imagined that his death would drive people to drink.

"Do you mind if I sit down?" I asked gently.

"Help yourself!" she exclaimed, nodding at the chair beside her. "You weren't in the competition, were you?"

"No, my friend was." I pointed to Juliet.

"Oh. Yeah. Are they done questioning her?"

"Yes. That's why I came over here. We wanted to know what they asked you."

"They peppered me with questions about where I baked the pie and where I got my ingredients. And what happened when I dropped the pie off? Did anyone have access to my pie before I brought it here? What are they not telling us?"

I was more nervous by the moment. Why would they ask these kinds of questions about a simple heart attack? Something was up.

"Ms. Daniel!" Sheriff Mack shouted across the room.

When I looked up, he gestured angrily at me. "I gotta go," I gave her an apologetic smile.

"What do you think you're doing?" he demanded when I stood in front of him.

"I was talking to Mabel."

"I can see that. About what?"

"I asked her if she was okay. Obviously, everyone is shaken."

"Is that all you asked?" he grunted.

This was very suspicious, and I didn't like it one bit. "I asked her what her conversation with you was like. What is going on? Why all the questions? Does the coroner think this is more than a heart attack?" I didn't want to believe Heidi when she said the coroner suspected LeClair was poisoned. That was ludicrous.

"Just go back to your lunch," he pointed to Wendy and Juliet, "and keep to yourself, okay?"

"Juliet is a friend, and when you treat her more like a suspect, it concerns me," I told him.

"Lunch!" he exclaimed before I spun on my heel, heading back to my friends, grumbling the entire way. On the one hand, he sent me out to solve cases he couldn't; on the other, he was constantly after me to mind my own business and leave it up to the professionals. I couldn't help it if I had special skills the others didn't.

I would have been perfectly happy as a hotel bartender living a perfectly normal life and not stumbling across bodies every other month. Some days, I wished I wasn't a ghost whisperer. I immediately felt guilty for even thinking that. I'd never have met Clara or Mystery. Juliet and Wendy and I wouldn't have the same relationship if I weren't. And I have seen and done some amazing things since I moved here. I just hated it when Surly Steve was so bossy. It always put me in a bad mood. Who did he think he was?

I flopped back down in my chair, picked up an onion ring from Wendy's plate, and stabbed at the ketchup with it.

"What?" I asked Wendy grumpily when I noticed her staring at me.

"I'm just wondering when you're finally going to admit you like him."

"Like him? Like him? He drives me crazy. I don't like him!"

"Whatever you say."

All heads in the bar turned when we heard a loud argument from the doorway. It was Daisy and her mother, and neither looked happy. "What did you tell them? I told you not to talk to them!" Daisy's mom berated her.

"I only told them what I know," Daisy cried.

"Why must you constantly disappoint me?" her mother asked again as nearly everyone in the bar cringed. That poor girl. No wonder she was always biting her nails. She was a nervous wreck. I hoped they were headed into the bar like everyone else so I could talk to Daisy as well, but my hopes were dashed when her mother grabbed her by the elbow and pulled her away after she noticed everyone staring at them.

I turned to Juliet, waiting for her to pick up on Wendy's teasing about the sheriff, but she still sat quietly, staring into space.

"Oh! Oh!" several people pointed to the TV above the bar when we saw the reporter outside the hotel.

"Turn it up!" Mabel demanded.

"Tragedy unfolded only a short time ago at the Red Castle Hotel during the Great Harvest Pie Showdown when famed television chef Sebastian LeClair collapsed after tasting a pumpkin pie submitted by a local baker..."

Juliet moaned, dropping her head into her hands.

"Sources believe the chef died from natural causes..."

"See!" Wendy exclaimed, patting Juliet on the back, who looked a bit brighter at the news.

"Wait," the reporter continued, "I'm getting breaking news..."

Oh dear. I didn't like the sound of that.

"Correction. My sources say it *wasn't* a heart attack or natural causes. We're told that Sebastian LeClair was poisoned."

SEVEN

Loud gasps rippled across the bar right before the reporter announced, "Warning. What you're about to see may upset some viewers." The broadcast cut to the coverage of LeClair pontificating about his own recipes right before taking a bite of Juliet's pie and collapsing. As if it couldn't get any worse, the camera swung to focus on Juliet's horrified expression.

Juliet watched this play out on TV, shock claiming her features, while Wendy threw her arm around her. What a disaster.

"It appears that the last bite Chef LeClair ever took was from the pie submitted by Juliet Beaumont of Sol Conceptions Bakery on Grand Avenue."

And it just got worse. Way worse.

"Authorities have assured us that the contestants are being questioned extensively..."

"I have to get out of here," Juliet whispered, her face changing from pale to green.

"I'll take you home, honey," Wendy said.

"I'll get the bill," I told her before she carefully led Juliet from the bar. "Call me if you need anything!" I insisted.

How did this nightmare happen? And what next? In that moment, I only knew three things for certain: Sebastian LeClair was dead, and it wasn't an accident, and Juliet didn't do it. The pie competition had turned into a murder investigation, and somehow, as usual, I was right in the middle of it.

"HEY GUYS, I'M HOME!" I announced when I walked into the house, hoping Clara hadn't seen the news.

"We saw the news!" Clara exclaimed the moment she saw me.

So much for breaking it to her gently.

"What a mess, huh?" I responded.

"Why did Juliet kill that chef guy?" Mystery asked.

"She didn't kill him. She didn't kill anybody!" I scolded.

"But her pie was the only one he ate right before he keeled over," Mystery pointed out.

"Obviously, I know that, but the poison could have come from anywhere! Someone could have poisoned his breakfast. Or his water. Or the golden fork. I don't know. I don't know anything yet. Except that Juliet didn't do it."

"Sheriff Mack doesn't think Juliet did it, right?" Clara asked.

"That's another thing I don't know. It's hard to say what he's thinking, but they questioned all the contestants for a long time and told them not to leave town."

"Oh, that's awful," Clara said, wringing her ghostly hands. "Does this mean Sheriff Mack might come to the house again? It's been a while," she mentioned hopefully.

"Let's hope it doesn't come to that," I said, rolling my eyes at Clara's disappointed expression. What did she see in him? Sure, he was good looking, and manly, and he smelled good, but that's the most I was willing to admit. He was annoying as all heck, and that was that.

I paced back and forth in the living room, dragging my fingers through my hair in frustration. Clara sat in her favorite armchair, her ghostly form slightly more translucent in the waning evening light, while Mystery lounged on the back of the couch, her tail swishing lazily.

"It just doesn't add up," I muttered, more to myself than anyone else. "Why would a big-shot celebrity chef like Sebastian LeClair suddenly move to Glenwood Springs? He claimed he wanted peace and quiet, but everything about the man still screamed attention-seeker." I stopped pacing and turned to face Clara and Mystery. "And now he's dead. Coincidence? I think not."

Clara nodded sagely. "In over 100 years, I know that people rarely do anything without a reason," she mused.

Mystery yawned. "Perhaps," she added, "the famous chef had a secret recipe he was trying to protect. Or hide."

I frowned in frustration. "You sound like Wendy. But whatever his reason was, you mark my words. It will be the key to solving his murder. I'm certain of it. I'm also certain I'll be digging into LeClair's skeletons."

"I don't think Sheriff Mack will appreciate that," Clara tsked.

"I'm sure he won't," I muttered.

"Now you're *certain* Juliet didn't kill the guy?" Mystery asked again.

"Yes!" Clara and I exclaimed.

"All right. All right. Sheez. No need to get testy over it," Mystery said before jumping down from the couch and stomping off, her tail swishing grumpily.

THE FOLLOWING MORNING, I went for my usual swim in the hot springs, and LeClair's murder was all anyone was talking about. Even one of the spirits who liked to follow me underwater as I did laps (boy, did he scare the heck out of me the first time I met him!) had heard the gossip.

Afterward, I headed to Sol Conceptions because Wendy texted me earlier that she had given Juliet a calming tea to help her sleep, but she was still distraught.

I pulled up to the bakery, surprised to find several empty parking spots directly in front of the bakery - usually, at this time of day, I'd have to circle the block at least twice or park down the street. My heart sank when I stepped out of my bus and peered through the window. The ordinarily bustling bakery was empty, save for Juliet slumped in a chair with Wendy trying to comfort her.

When the bell chimed as I entered, Juliet looked up hopefully but slumped again when she realized it was only me. "Hey, ladies," I said softly. I would have asked how it was going, but it was clear it wasn't going well at all.

"Hey, Holly," Wendy said, jumping up and hugging me.

"What's happening here?" I asked, even though I could already guess.

"People think I killed LeClair!" Juliet gasped. "And the cops think I killed him!"

"I'm sure that's not true," I insisted. "Everyone knows you and loves you and would never think in a million years you were capable of that. If anyone would be a murderer, it would be me, right," I joked, hoping to lighten the mood but to no avail.

"Then how do you explain this?" she sobbed, thrusting a piece of paper in my direction.

"What is it?" I asked.

"It was slipped through the mail slot overnight."

MURDERER!

was written in thick block letters. Didn't people have better things to do?

"You should turn this over to the police," I urged her.

"What good would that do?" she lamented.

"Maybe they could check for fingerprints," I suggested.

"Why would they look for fingerprints?"

"Because the real murderer might have written this!"

When Juliet glared at me like I'd gone completely bonkers, I realized how ridiculous that sounded. I was only trying to help but I was grasping at straws here. Someone murdered LeClair, and it looked like they used Juliet's pie to do it.

When the bell over the door jingled again, we spun around, hoping to see a new customer. I inadvertently groaned when I realized it was Sheriff Mack.

"Good morning to you, too," he said, staring grumpily at me.

It was nothing personal. I was just hoping it was a customer. Or ten. Okay, maybe it was a bit personal. Why must he aggravate me so?

"Ms. Beaumont, I have some follow-up questions for you," he said, waiting for Wendy and me to give them privacy. Of course, neither Wendy nor I budged.

"They can stay," Juliet sighed.

"Can you tell me if you have access to wolfsbane?"

"Wolfsbane?" Wendy shrieked. "LeClair was poisoned with wolfsbane?"

The sheriff threw Wendy an annoyed look. "It was found in his bloodwork," he responded. "*And*, in Ms. Beaumont's pie."

With that, Juliet sat down so quickly I was worried she might faint.

"Does wolfsbane normally work that fast?" I asked. Whenever someone was poisoned with it on TV, it took a while. Of course, that was TV, and this was real life, so what did I know?

"It's possible," Wendy pointed out. "Given LeClair's lack of, er, well, fitness, it might have worked faster on him than on a younger, healthier person."

"Since you brought it up, I have to ask if *you* have access to wolfsbane," Sheriff Mack said, staring at Wendy.

"Why are you asking her?" I demanded.

"I'm just trying to cover all my bases," he replied, throwing up his hands.

"Oh yeah! Well, cover this!" I insisted, waving the note Juliet received in front of him.

"What is this?" he asked.

"Someone slipped it into her mailbox overnight!" I told him, getting madder by the moment. I was infuriated that anyone could think my friend was a murderer.

"I'll look into it," he said calmly.

"You better not be singling out my friends because they're witches!" I exclaimed, taking another step toward him while glaring daggers at him.

"Sit down, Ms. Daniel, or I'll take you to the station for interfering with an investigation."

"It's okay, Holly," Juliet sighed. "The last thing I need right now is my friend getting arrested."

"It's often used as a repellent against werewolves," Wendy pointed out. "I know some people who keep it in their gardens to protect their homes."

"I've never even seen real wolfsbane, much less kept it on hand," Juliet said. "Why would I?"

"What about you?" he asked Wendy. "You still haven't answered my question."

"I don't even know what it looks like," I interrupted. What if I had some growing in my garden and didn't know it?

"It's this gorgeous helmet-shaped purple flower," Wendy said, holding her hands in a circle. "It can grow right through the fall while all the other plants have died out for the season. And you shouldn't touch it. You could get poisoned just by coming in contact with it," she explained. "And no," she said, looking the sheriff right in the eye, "I don't have any."

"Can you tell me where you were at 1:00 yesterday afternoon?" Sheriff Mack asked Juliet.

"1:00? Um. Well. I was getting ready for the competition."

"But where *were* you?"

"Why are you asking this?" I butted in again.

"Ms. Daniel, if you don't stop interrupting me, I'll make you wait in my car until I'm done here."

I folded my arms and glared at him anyway.

"Ms. Beaumont, where were you at 1:00?"

"I was on my way to the Red Castle Hotel."

"Driving? Walking?"

"I drove there. Why? What is this all about?"

"Are you sure you weren't at the hotel already?"

"I'm sure. I had an anniversary cake to deliver to a customer, so I ran a bit late."

"We have a tipster who claimed they saw you sneaking around the hotel kitchen, which was off limits to contestants, at 1:00, which, as you know, was shortly before the competition started."

"That's not true. I swear."

"We also have a witness who overheard you, in this bakery, saying repeatedly that you'd do '*anything* to win.' They also noted you were upset upon learning that LeClair was added as a judge and that you planned to change your pie recipe because of it. Perhaps you accidentally added something you shouldn't have in your haste?"

"I said that because I wanted to beat Mabel Winchester, not because I was willing to poison someone to do it! That was taken out of context!" Juliet protested.

"You know what? You can lock me in your sheriff's car all you want," I snapped at him, "but Juliet, you don't have to answer these questions."

"That's all right. I'm done here," Sheriff Mack claimed. "But what I told you yesterday still applies to all of you. Don't leave town," he grunted, waving a finger at each of us.

With that, he spun on his heel and walked to the door while I made a face behind his back.

"I saw that!" he claimed as he opened the door for a young man wearing a courier uniform.

"Good morning! Welcome to Sol Conceptions!" Juliet said, trying her best to sound enthusiastic. But how could she be excited about anything when she just had a grilling about a murder?

"I have a package for a Juliet Beaumont."

"Oh," she responded, looking so disappointed that it broke my heart. "That's me."

The courier handed her the package before leaving abruptly.

"What is this? I wasn't expecting a delivery," Juliet said, turning the package over before opening it.

"Who's it from?" I asked.

"It doesn't say." She shrugged while tugging on the tab of the padded envelope. When she pulled out three purple flowers wrapped in plastic, she screamed and dropped them.

"Wolfsbane!" Wendy exclaimed.

EIGHT

A CHAIN OF CLUES

"Don't touch it!" Wendy insisted, holding her arms up to keep Juliet and me from moving. "Do you have metal tongs?" she asked.

"Of course," Juliet said, pointing to the counter next to the cash register. While Wendy went to fetch the tongs, Juliet and I gawked at each other in horror. Someone just sent poison to her bakery. The same poison used to kill Sebastian LeClair.

After using the tongs to place the flowers back in the shipping package, Wendy muttered an incantation I didn't understand and declared the package safe to handle for now, but we still weren't to touch the flowers directly.

"I don't feel comfortable keeping those in the bakery," Juliet said.

"This advice will shock you," I told her, "but you should turn these over to Sheriff Mack."

"Won't it make her look guilty?" Wendy asked. "We all just swore that we don't have any wolfsbane, but five minutes later, oops, sorry, here's some of the poisonous plant you asked about?"

"Normally, I would agree," I explained. "You know I'm not one to run to the sheriff with everything I learn about a case, but he saw the courier, and we have the package addressed to Juliet..." I trailed off.

"Holly is right," Juliet said. "This is too dangerous not to tell Surly Steve. Why would anyone send me this, to begin with?" she asked.

"Someone is setting you up," I insisted.

"Holly's right," Wendy agreed with a nod.

"But why? I mean, why *me*?"

"That's what we have to figure out," I told her. "Consider the possibility that someone paid a courier to deliver it while the sheriff was here, forcing you to confess to having it in the bakery."

"But the courier showed up just as the sheriff was leaving. If someone did it on purpose, their timing was off."

"I didn't say I had all the answers," I pointed out. "It's still a working theory."

"Dude, that's scary," Wendy whispered while Juliet nodded tearfully.

"I know I must sound like a broken record, but I'm still convinced LeClair's move to Glenwood is suspicious and should be the focus of our investigation."

"But how?" Wendy asked.

"Let's start with the pie competition contestants and work our way from there."

"Do you want me to come with you?" Juliet asked.

"No, you call Surly Steve and tell him to come back and pick up the package. Otherwise, you should act like everything is perfectly normal and you're completely innocent."

"But I *am* completely innocent," Juliet pointed out.

"Obviously, I know that. But I want others to think it as well. Do either of you know where LeClair was living? Did he buy a house? Was he renting? The first I saw of him was when he flattened me at the pool."

"Daisy told me he was staying at the Red Castle Hotel for now," Juliet said.

"Daisy Thompson, that nervous contestant whose mom wouldn't stop nagging her?"

"Yes, that's her."

"How did she know where Sebastian was staying?" I asked.

Juliet shook her head. "I'm not sure. She told me while we were waiting for the competition to start. And now that you mention it, I saw them having what looked like a serious discussion when I dropped off my pie."

"Serious discussion?" I asked. "Like an argument?"

"I couldn't tell for sure." Juliet shrugged. "But it didn't look friendly. I got the sense he was lecturing her."

"Hmmm. Well!" I clapped my hands together. "I'll go to the hotel to see what I can learn from the ghosts, and you hit the internet," I insisted, pointing at Wendy. "Check out social media accounts, TMZ, Page Six, dig up any New York gossip on LeClair that you can find. And you," I hugged Juliet, "stay here, call Sheriff Mack to come get the wolfsbane, *and* keep the faith, okay? We're on this!"

Juliet nodded grimly. "I'll do the best I can."

WENDY ZIPPED away on her mint green Vespa while I drove straight to the Red Castle Hotel. It's ridiculous that Sheriff Mack or anyone who has known Juliet for more than five minutes could even entertain the idea that she'd murder anyone. She's the kind of person who takes spiders outside and wishes them well on their journey.

Once inside the hotel, I headed straight for the third floor in the east wing, where I was sure I'd find one of my best spirit sources for hotel gossip: Betty, the chain-smoking maid from Atlanta. She worked for the hotel throughout the 60s and 70s but died during a night shift in 1981. That night, she was extra tired and lay down on a hotel bed for a nap but never woke up.

One of her favorite pastimes was playing pranks on the guests. "They come for ghosts, I give em' ghosts," she liked to say. Sure enough, I found Betty messing with some guests by pushing the buttons next to the elevator. When the guest pushed up, she pushed down. The guests thought the elevator was malfunctioning and talked about taking the stairs.

"Betty!" I exclaimed with exasperation, which made the already freaked out couple nearly jump out of their skin. "Get over here!"

The guests were so confused they didn't know what to do. "Please excuse us," I told them while they continued staring at me awkwardly.

Betty finally approached me, laughing uproariously before lapsing into a coughing fit.

"Do you smell cigarettes?" the husband asked the wife.

"You too?" she said. "I thought this was a non-smoking hotel."

"It's supposed to be. I'm complaining to the front desk!"

"You do that!" Betty laughed again before taking a big puff on the permanent cigarette dangling from her hand and blowing smoke in their direction.

She wore her hair styled with the 'feathered' look popular in her day, while her uniform was a crisp, light blue dress that fell just above her knees with short sleeves and a white Peter Pan collar. A matching blue belt cinched the dress at her waist, and the name Betty was embroidered on the left side of her chest. A small white apron tied around her waist included pockets bulging with cleaning supplies and hotel amenities.

"What's up, girl?" she asked me, after another coughing fit. "I really gotta cut back," she said, laughing some more.

"What can you tell me about Sebastian LeClair?"

"The dude who croaked after eating your friend's pie?" she asked, lifting an eyebrow at me.

"Yes, that's the one."

"Boy, was he a--"

"Betty!" I exclaimed before she said something I was certain one shouldn't say in public.

"What? It's not like anyone but you can hear me."

"So we agree, he was a piece of work. Got any juicy secrets for me, though?"

"Oh, honey," she drawled, a plume of blue smoke curling around her head, "that LeClair fella was jumpier than a long-tailed cat in a room full of rocking chairs." She took another long drag of her cigarette before continuing. "Always peeking 'round corners, like he expected the bogeyman to pop out."

"Would you say he came here because he was looking to slow down, leave the city life behind, and embrace our slow mountain town way of life?"

Betty laughed again. "I've been dead long enough to smell a rat. That man didn't come here for no R&R, I'll tell you that much. He was hiding something or hiding from someone. Mark my words," she said, pointing her cigarette toward me.

"Any other ghosts who may have witnessed his strange behavior?"

"Charles seemed particularly interested in him."

"Where is he?"

"Hey Charles! The breather wants to talk to you!" she bellowed.

"Was that really necessary?" I cringed, placing my hands over my ears.

"How else was I gonna git him?" she asked like it was such a ridiculous question.

"What's up?" Charles said, nodding at me. Charles was a pudgy, balding spirit who worked in hotel maintenance. Until the day he accidentally electrocuted himself. His fingertips were blackened, and I swore sometimes I smelled singed hair when he was around.

"She wants to know more about that LeClair fella."

"Oh, yeah, he was weird."

"Weird, how?"

"We all agreed he was up to something," Charles responded, while Betty nodded. "He was nervous, always looking over his shoulder."

"That's it?" I asked.

"I think so." Charles shrugged. "What more did you want?"

"It's just that it isn't much to go on, but I guess it's something."

"Oh, hey, I remember he was yelling at one of the pie-baking contestants in the kitchen the night before he died."

"Really?" I said excitedly. "Which one?"

"The one with the glasses."

"Eliot Thornfield?"

"Yeah, I think that's him," Charles responded.

"What was he yelling about?"

"He said the guy wasn't supposed to be in there. None of the contestants were. Told him he could kick him out of the competition if he saw him in there again. You know what you should do? Check with the kitchen ghosts and staff. They might have seen or overheard something," Betty suggested.

"That's a great idea. I'll do that right now!" I told her.

"No problem," she said before she and Charles faded away, off to haunt some more guests, I assumed.

The hotel kitchen was its usual hive of activity, sounds, and scents. Cooks in crisp white uniforms darted between stainless steel counters, their knives flashing as they chopped vegetables and carved meats with practiced precision. The air was thick with the aroma of sizzling garlic, roasting meats, and sweet desserts. Servers weaved through the organized chaos, balancing trays laden with artfully plated dishes destined for eager diners in the restaurant beyond.

Several employees and ghosts greeted me as they passed by, and I realized how lucky I was that my employee ID got me into places most people couldn't go. It also made me one of them, so the staff weren't on their guard like they would be if I were a sheriff's deputy.

I approached one of the bussers, who was perched on a stool, scrolling through his phone and drinking a pop.

"Hi, Tim."

"Hi, Holly, I didn't know you were working today."

"I'm not. I just have a few questions about what happened here yesterday."

"A guy died!"

"Yes, I realize that. Did you see or hear anything suspicious?"

Tim crooked his head. "Like what?"

"Anything out of the ordinary? Anything weird?"

"No, I don't think so. Yo, Bernie!" he called out to a server.

"Holly needs to know if you saw anything suspicious yesterday before that guy died."

Bernie shook his head. "The cops already asked us that."

"I'm sure they did," I told him. "I'm just following up. In case anyone forgot that they saw something."

"Didn't you tell me you saw one of the contestants snooping around in here before the contest started?" Tim asked.

"Oh yeah, I did."

"Who was it? Which one?" I pressed him.

"No clue."

"You saw someone, but you don't know which one?"

"I mean, I don't know her name."

"Her. Can you describe her?" My heart raced. Oh, please don't describe Juliet, please!

"She was a big lady with gray hair and a tight bun on her head," he said, pointing to the back of his head for emphasis.

Thank goodness! "That would be Mabel," I told him. "What was she doing?"

"I couldn't tell you for sure. I came in to get water for a guest, and I saw her next to the fridge. They told us not to let anyone back here before the competition, and it looked like she was snooping around, so I asked her what she was doing. She said she was checking on the pies to make sure they were secure. She didn't want anyone cheating, you know. Sorry, I can't be of more help."

"No, that's great! Thank you. You've been very helpful. I was also wonder-- oops. Hang on." My phone buzzed with a text. It was Wendy.

Get over to the bookstore right away. You won't believe what I found!

NINE
CAUGHT ON CAMERA

Wendy's bookstore was only a block from the Red Castle Hotel, which is how we met. I was wandering along 6th Street and thought her store was awfully cute, so I popped in for a book about Glenwood Springs to learn more about the town I just moved to.

Her urgent message just now had me jogging there. I desperately hoped somehow she found our killer and this would all be over quickly. I felt at least somewhat vindicated by what the ghosts told me. No way LeClair was here to retire. It was for darker reasons, and I had to uncover them.

As usual, Wendy had decorated the storefront for fall. She draped garlands of vibrant autumn leaves and twinkling fairy lights across the picture window while a display of pumpkins in various sizes and shades - from deep orange to ghostly white lined the sidewalk. Several small tables sat out front, encouraging shoppers to stick around and read while sipping a steaming cup of hot apple cider. It was like stepping into the pages of a cozy autumn tale it was so quaint, but I barely noticed it today. I was too eager to learn what she found.

"I'm here!" I exclaimed, bursting through the door, making the bell above jingle wildly.

MEOW! One of the cats bellowed while sprinting behind the counter.

"Hey! Watch it!" Wendy complained. "You scared Roo."

"Sorry, Roo!" I called after him. "I didn't realize you were right there. What is that?" I asked when I spotted a mangled pile of orange yarn next to the cash register.

"Rabbit didn't care for his latest sweater," she said.

"Imagine that. Now, quick, what did you find?"

"Check it out," Wendy said, pointing to her computer monitor and pushing play on a video.

It was a heated argument between Sebastian LeClair and Mabel Winchester at the Saturday morning Farmer's Market.

"That's Mabel!" I exclaimed so loudly that another one of the cats, sunning himself in the window, I wasn't sure which one, they all looked alike to me, got up and stomped off.

"If you don't stop startling my cats, you'll have to leave," Wendy said crossly.

"I'm so sorry you guys!" I was used to Mystery, who wasn't easily startled. Easily offended, sure. But startled? Not so much. Except when Sheriff Mack came to the house. She'd shout "popo" and run and hide. I told her that wasn't very nice and stop calling him that. She asked what was the difference, he couldn't hear her after all.

The video started shaky, like the person filming it grabbed their phone in the middle of the drama and didn't want to miss anything. Mabel stood behind the table at her stall, hands on hips, her face red, her tight bun starting to come undone while Sebastian sniffed one of her jam jars.

"Merde! What a joke! I can smell the artificial flavors in this," he insisted.

"How dare you!" Mabel shouted. "I'll have you know that all of my ingredients are natural and locally sourced right here in Colorado."

"No, they're not." Sebastian scoffed before slamming the jar down on the table.

"You wouldn't know the difference between real food and your fancy-schmancy molecular gastronomy nonsense if it jumped up and bit you--."

"Ha! I'll have you know I trained at Le Cordon Bleu, and this..." he sneered, sweeping his hand over her table, "is nothing but peasant food. And magical? Ha!"

"You may have trained at Le Cordon Bleu, but you know what? You've clearly lost touch with true flavors after all your years of playing a chef on TV."

"Watch it, or I'll get you thrown out of the pie competition and then expose you for the fraud you are," he growled menacingly.

"You can't do that!" she protested.

"Oh, can't I?"

Mabel's eyes flashed dangerously, "You don't know who you're messing with, mister!" At that, Sebastian stormed off, but not before Mabel could work in another shot. "You'll get your just *desserts*, LeClair! Mark my words! You'll wish the only thing you *thought* you tasted were artificial ingredients."

"Whoa!" I responded.

"You see why I told you to get over here asap?"

"This is huge. I have to see Mabel," I said, spinning on my heel, prepared to sprint all the way to her shop if I had to. But before I could take another step, Sheriff Mack, of all people, walked in the door and wasn't the least bit surprised to see us together. But just as he opened his mouth to lecture us, Eeyore streaked over the tops of his shoes and darted into a book stack.

"Why is that cat still naked?" he asked.

I bit my lip to keep from laughing, knowing we'd also been through the naked cat argument with him before.

"Peas in a pod, huh?" Wendy glared at us. "You know very well they aren't naked! They're hairless!"

"It seriously doesn't grow back? I thought you were kidding when you told me about them the first time."

I was dying inside. Just dying.

"I told you to watch the Austin Powers movie!" Wendy demanded.

"Austin, what?" Sheriff Mack responded in confusion.

"Ugh. I still think," she started, and I didn't care for the gleam in her eye, "you too should see the movie together!"

"I fail to see how that will explain your naked cats," the sheriff responded.

"Just watch it. You could make it a date," she insisted while Sheriff Mack and I rolled our eyes at each other.

"I assume you didn't come here to complain about Wendy's naked cats, but I have something to tell you," I insisted.

"It better not be about my case," he said.

"Uhhh."

"That's what I thought. I came here to ask you both about the wolfsbane delivered to Sol Conceptions this morning. You're sure it's safe to handle the package?"

"Yes," Wendy explained. "The package is perfectly safe, thanks to my spell, but only a trained technician should handle the plant."

"And you two swear that the courier I let into the bakery is the one who dropped off the package?"

"Yes!" we answered simultaneously.

"And what did you need to tell me?" he asked.

"I was just at the hotel questioning some of the ghosts," I started.

"I'm sure you were."

It helped that he knew about my ghost whispering gifts. It took some persuading at first, but eventually, he gave in. Heck, it even took some persuading on my part to tell him. After a lifetime of denying them, It was almost instinct to hide my abilities.

"One of the ghosts, Betty, told me that Sebastian LeClair was always nervous and on edge. Always looking over his shoulder."

"Go on," he said, squaring his stance and crossing his arms over his broad chest, which he often did when I annoyed him. Sometimes, Wendy, Juliet, and I imitated him behind his back. To be fair, I could only imagine what he must say about *us* back at the station.

"Another ghost, Charles, said he overheard LeClair kicking one of the contestants, Eliot Thornfield, out of the kitchen the night before the contest.

"And?"

"And what?"

"Is that it? Is that all you have?" he grunted.

"Well, yes, for now, but I'm sure I'll get more."

"And what am I supposed to do with this so-called information?"

"You have to follow up! My gut says LeClair was here because he was hiding from something or someone."

"And that's relevant how?" Sheriff Mack asked.

"It proves Juliet didn't kill him!"

"The only thing it *might* prove at this point is that he was kind of a weird guy. I must tell you, ladies, that it isn't looking good for your friend."

"There's no way you think Juliet killed anyone," I insisted.

"I follow the evidence, and right now, the evidence points to Juliet."

"Well, then, why haven't you arrested her?" I shot back, much to Wendy's horror.

"Because. At this point, the evidence is circumstantial, and I don't have a motive. But if I find more, I *will* arrest her. Got it?"

"Wendy, show him what you found on social media!" I urged.

"Here, watch!" Wendy said.

"I was researching LeClair's background..." Wendy started while I shook my head at her. "I mean, I coincidentally stumbled across this video..."

"No doubt," Sheriff Mack bit back sarcastically.

"Look. See for yourself." Wendy played the video where Mabel and Sebastian were arguing.

"That proves nothing," he pointed out.

"But it's suspicious. And, I'd like to add, when I talked to the kitchen staff--"

He sighed heavily. "When did you talk to the kitchen staff? And why?"

When I opened my mouth to explain, he held up his hand, "Never mind. I obviously know why you were talking to them. Go ahead."

"I asked them if anyone noticed anything suspicious, and one of the servers told me he saw Mabel in the kitchen even though they told everyone it was strictly off limits before the contest."

"Did Mabel tell him why she was in there?"

"She claimed she was checking on the pies. Making sure they were secure."

"You don't believe that?" he pressed.

"Not after that video! Don't you think you should check this out?"

"What I think is, I'd like to get on with my day and not have to follow you around. If that's all, I have to go," he said before heading out the door. "And please, leave this investigation to the professionals."

The moment the door closed behind him, I announced to Wendy. "I have to talk to Mabel."

But then the door opened a crack, and the sheriff stuck his head in. "No, you don't need to talk to Mabel. Stay out of my investigation," he said, while Wendy and I stared at each other in awe. How did he do that?

After he closed the door, we watched it, waiting for it to open again so he could lecture us some more.

When it didn't, I whispered to Wendy, "I'm outta here!"

TEN

A TASTE OF DECEPTION

Tucked into the corner of 2nd and Laurel Street, Mabel's Magical Preserves was a small and vibrant purple shop with window frames painted glittering gold that winked and sparkled in the sunlight. Hand-drawn vines and berries snaked up the sides of the building while the sign on the door showed *Welcome We're Open!*

When I stepped into the store, the scent of sugar, spice, and something indefinably enchanting greeted me. Jewel-toned jars representing every imaginable fruit lined the shelves. Strawberries and peaches, of course, along with exotic mountain berries and herbs known only to those who venture deep into the surrounding forests.

A selection of her prized creations sat on a special display in the center of the shop: shimmering jars of "Moonlight Marmalade," which served as a protection against werewolves, containers of "Whisper Wish Raspberry Jam" that, when I put my ear close to it seemed to hum softly, and next to that her notorious "Love Potion Plum Preserves" that included a warning label about potential side effects.

In one corner, a small sitting area allowed visitors to

sample the daily special, served on delicate china. The walls were adorned with old family photos, pressed herbs, and the occasional "First Place" ribbon from the county fair - though some visitors swore the ribbons changed color when no one was looking.

"I'll be right with you!" Mabel called out while ringing up a customer's purchase at the cash register.

"No problem," I told her.

After several moments of reassuring the customer that her lucky jam was sure to bring her good fortune on tomorrow's job interview, Mabel joined me across the shop. "How can I help you?" she asked. "Oh, that's one of our most popular," she cooed when she saw me examining a jar of sour cherry preserves.

"It looks really good."

"Would you like to try a sample?" she asked.

"Sure. Why not?" I responded.

"I have an open jar in the back. I'll get you some crackers, too," she explained before hurrying to the back room. She returned in short order with a small, round silver tray stacked with some water crackers, a small bowl of preserves, and a jam spreader.

"Weren't you at the pie competition when Sebastian LeClair died?" I asked as if it had just now occurred to me. I hoped she didn't recall our brief conversation at the bar.

"I was!" she said, raising a skeptical eyebrow. "Were you in the audience?"

"Yes, but it must have been especially scary for you to have been sitting so close to the victim."

"You want the truth?" she whispered, leaning in close.

"Yes!" I said, wondering what she was about to confess.

"That guy was a jerk. And a liar. I'd bet that a lot of people secretly think he got what he deserved. Besides, I'm annoyed that the contest was cut short like that. I was sure to win again this year. Did you know I've won three years in a row? And this would have made four!"

"Well, if your pie was anything like these preserves, you were a shoo-in!" I exclaimed.

"I certainly think so!" she said.

"What kind of pie did you make?"

"Pecan. But I guess it could be worse. At least I'm not being accused of murder, right?" she said with a nervous laugh.

"Why did you say a lot of people would be happy he died? Did you know him personally?"

"I didn't *know* him, but that didn't stop him from claiming my preserves were made from artificial ingredients. And that I was a fraud!"

"He did not!" I responded in mock indignation.

"He sure did. At the Farmer's Market. I've never been so insulted in my life."

"Now that I think of it, I'm pretty sure I saw that on video."

"Video? What video? There's a video?" she asked, verging on panic.

"Your argument with LeClair at the farmer's market. Someone posted it on social media."

"What's on this video?" she demanded, sounding increasingly less confident. No doubt wondering if her threats about *just desserts* were recorded. I'd argue that her statement she was glad he was dead was almost a confession itself.

"It's right here!" I pulled up the video on my phone, holding it up for her to watch.

Mabel's face transformed from confusion to shock, then to a mix of defiance and embarrassment, her cheeks flushing a deep red as she saw herself on the small screen of my phone, arguing with LeClair and threatening him.

"You even threatened him at the end," I pointed out to drive my point home. "Not that I blame you, of course. He didn't seem like a very nice man."

"Clearly, I was upset," she stammered, her voice getting shrill and loud. "I'd never harm anyone."

"But what did you mean when you said he'd get his just desserts? Kind of weird, don't you think that he died after eating pie."

"I didn't mean anything by that. I was angry. People say things in the heat of the moment. Haven't you ever said something you regretted because you were angry?"

"I have," I had to admit. It still didn't make her any less of a killer.

"See!" she chortled.

"But here's the other thing. I was at the Red Castle Hotel earlier today, and one of the servers told me that he saw you in the kitchen right before the contest started, even though the rules specifically stated none of the contestants were allowed back there."

"Why were you talking to a server about me? Who are you?" she demanded while picking up the sample tray and moving away. "And why was he saying I was in the kitchen when I wasn't supposed to be?"

"So you weren't in the kitchen before the judging started?"

She paused her retreat to the back of the store. "Oh, you know, I just remembered I went there to check on the pies.- Make sure they were secure, you know? Wouldn't want anyone cheating..." she trailed off. She was clearly torn between trying to make excuses for herself and making a beeline for the back of the store where she could hide.

"Did you suspect someone might cheat?" I asked, following her.

"Those rumors about me are complete fabrications!" she exclaimed.

"Rumors?" I asked. "What rumors?" Her expression told me that slipped out.

"Oh, it's nothing." She waved her hand dismissively. "Just some jealous people who were convinced that after winning three years in a row, I must be cheating."

"So, you weren't?"

"Who are you again?" she demanded, her face turning dark as she finally realized I didn't just wander in here to sample her jams.

"I'm Holly Daniel. I'm a Paranormal Private Investigator."

"You work for the cops?" she asked, pinching her lips in disdain.

"Nope. I'm only wondering who could have poisoned Sebastian LeClair."

"Well, it certainly wasn't me! And now, if you don't mind, I have work to do. In fact, there's another customer," she insisted as a new customer conveniently came into the shop. Perhaps Mabel's lucky jam was working its magic for her.

"Yes, of course." I nodded. That was unfortunate. I wanted to continue questioning her, but if I had, I might have been wearing the cherry preserves rather than tasting them.

As I left the shop, I pondered her reactions. Why was she in the hotel kitchen when she wasn't supposed to be? Was she poisoning Juliet's pie? As a witch and a jam cook, she could have had access to wolfsbane and would know how it worked.

On top of that, not only did LeClair accuse her of being a fraud, but she was suspected of cheating in the past. If what LeClair said was true, and he exposed her, her business could be ruined. Even though *I* doubted his so-called ability to detect freshness in ingredients, Mabel may not have. Someone who had built an entire business and reputation on local, fresh ingredients with magical properties would have way more motive than Juliet, who had no motive if you asked me.

"Fancy seeing you here," Sheriff Mack said when I nearly bumped into him on the sidewalk. Dangit. I really had to pay more attention when I was walking.

"What do you mean?" I asked, scowling at him. "I was just here shopping," I said, pointing to the shop next to us, which I didn't realize was vacant until I saw the huge "For Lease" sign in the window.

"You're shopping for storefront property?" he asked.

"Maybe. You never know. I could use an office."

When he gave me *that* look, I threw up my hands. "Fine. I was talking to Mabel," I confessed. That's obviously where he was headed as well, and he'd soon figure it out anyway. "Who, by the way, has far more motive than Juliet does."

"And how much motive does Juliet have?" he asked with an annoying smirk.

"None!" I exclaimed. "She has none! Well?" I demanded, hands on my hips, waiting for him to see this as vital as I did.

"Well, what?"

"You have to confront Mabel."

"I need to do my job, and you need to do *your* job. Whatever that is. And stay out of my investigation."

"You know darn well what my job is. Considering you pay me to help investigate paranormal cases."

"Exactly. We pay you as a consultant on cases where I specifically request your help. I haven't requested your help with this case, and I've ordered you to stay out of it."

"But you are here to talk to Mabel, right?"

"I am."

"About the video that Wendy found?" I asked, realizing I had him.

"Among other things."

"You have a nice day then, Sheriff," I said quickly, walking away before he could lecture me again.

"Stay out of my case!" he shouted at my retreating back.

My next stop was Sol Conceptions because I realized I had failed to follow up with Juliet about the sudden change in the competition testing order. Aside from LeClair dying after tasting her pie, that had to be the other reason Sheriff Mack saw her as the primary suspect. I only hoped *she* hadn't requested the change!

ELEVEN
A WRITER'S ALIBI

"Juliet!" I called out when I entered the bakery, disappointed to see it was still empty.

"I'm in the back!" she shouted.

I wandered that way, where I found her organizing a supply cupboard. "Whatcha doin'?" I asked, trying to keep the mood light.

"As long as I don't have any customers, I might as well catch up on some cleaning and organizing," she responded glumly.

"Still quiet, huh?"

"Yes, ma'am. Quiet as a church mouse."

"You'll be pleased to know that Wendy found a video on social media of Mabel threatening LeClair."

"Seriously? For what?" she asked, suddenly interested in what I had to say.

"He accused her of using artificial ingredients in her preserves and of being a fraud."

"No! She must have been furious."

"She told him not only would he get his just *desserts*, but that he'd wish the only thing he thought he tasted were artificial ingredients."

Juliet's jaw dropped. "What if she poisoned my pie?"

"She could have! A server at the hotel saw her sneaking around the kitchen right before the contest."

"Does Sheriff Mack know this?"

"He sure does. Although he wasn't exactly happy that I'm the one who discovered all of that," I admitted.

"What if LeClair was right? What if her ingredients aren't what she claims? And what if the rumors she cheated in the past are true? She could have been in the kitchen trying to cheat again. There's her motive!"

"There's a lot of herbs in her shop," I said. "And she offers an enchanted jam that protects against werewolves."

"I bet she would know about wolfsbane!" Juliet exclaimed. For the first time in two days, I saw actual hope in her eyes. "And you told Sheriff Mack all of this?"

"I did."

"What did he say? Is he going to check it out?"

"As usual, he kind of dismissed me. But he was at least interested enough to question her about it," I said, holding up my crossed fingers. "But of course, *I'll* keep looking into it. But now I have a question for you. You were surprised when they said there was a change in the tasting order?"

Juliet nodded vigorously.

My heart skipped a beat. What if Mabel was supposed to go first but insisted Juliet go instead because she slipped poison into her pie? "Who was supposed to go first originally? Was it Mabel?"

"That's a good question. But I don't actually know. They told me that morning that I was going last."

"Who said that?" I pressed.

"The event committee that oversees the whole thing."

"We need to find out who they scheduled to go first originally. Is there someone on the committee you could ask?"

"I could certainly try," she said.

"How did it go when you turned over the wolfsbane to Sheriff Mack? Did he grill you?"

"No." She shook her head. "He was surprisingly chill about it. He told me to be on alert and that he'd increase patrols around the bakery. If I see anything that looks suspicious, I'm to call him right away."

"He can't possibly think you murdered Sebastian LeClair."

"He didn't say anything about that." She shrugged. "All I know is the townspeople are definitely suspicious and avoiding me and the bakery."

"Well, I'm not avoiding your bakery, and I saw a delicious croissant out front that was calling my name."

"Help yourself," Juliet sighed heavily. "I don't want them to go to waste."

When I headed out to the dining area, Juliet followed.

"Should I make us some coffee?" I asked.

"I can do it. I need to keep my mind busy."

I put a croissant on a plate and sat near the cash register. "So tell me about the other contestants. I've already talked to Mabel, but what about the rest? Like this Eliot Thornfield guy? One of the hotel spirits saw LeClair kicking him out of the kitchen. And Wendy said he's new in town because he's here writing a book on the history of Glenwood."

"I don't know much about him," Juliet explained as she sat at the table with two cups of coffee. "But he seems eager to get involved with the community."

"Too eager?" I asked.

Juliet shrugged. "Yeah, maybe. He just seems a bit off to me, you know? But I can't quite put my finger on it."

"Do you think he's joining the events because it gives him more material for his book? Or something else?"

"Virginia, the librarian, was here last week with a friend, and I overheard them talking about him. She said he was in the library a lot doing research, but he asked strange questions."

"Strange questions, how?" I pressed.

"She said she got the distinct impression he didn't quite know what he was doing."

"But Wendy said he was a bestselling author," I reminded her.

"That's just it. The librarian looked him up and couldn't find anything he'd written. Not under Eliot Thornfield anyway."

"So maybe he writes under a pen name?"

"She asked him about that, but at first, he brushed her off. And when he gave her another name, she couldn't locate that one either."

"Maybe he's a ghostwriter? Writes best-selling books but for others and isn't allowed to reveal who it is?"

"Maybe," Juliet agreed.

"Is he staying at the Red Castle too? Like Sebastian?" I asked.

"No, I heard he rented this run down cottage at the edge of the town."

"The one that backs to the forest?"

"Yeah, that's it."

"Well, that's not creepy at all." I grimaced.

"Perhaps he wanted to be left alone to write?" Juliet suggested.

Juliet. Always the voice of reason. And me, always the one jumping to suspicious conclusions.

"I have to talk to him," I announced.

"Be careful, Holly. It's one thing to question Mabel in her shop when others are around. It's entirely another to drive out to the middle of nowhere to confront a stranger and ask him if he's a killer." Juliet wasn't just the voice of reason, she was the cautious one, too. But she wasn't wrong.

"How about this, I could talk to the librarian instead. See if she remembers any more details."

"I think that would be okay."

"I'll go as soon as I finish this delicious croissant!" I declared.

DURING MY DRIVE to the library, I worried about Juliet. I've never seen her so subdued. She was the one who always worried about us. But she was so quiet today. I shuddered to think what would happen if she actually got arrested for LeClair's murder. Would Sheriff Mack really do that? I didn't know how much say he had over these kinds of things.

What if the community pressured him to make an arrest because somehow they were convinced Juliet did it? I couldn't imagine that poor girl in prison. Not even for a moment. Nope. It was on me to solve this. I had to save my best friend.

I shivered as I approached the library steps, wrapping my light jacket tighter around me. The crisp autumn air nipped at my cheeks, carrying the earthy scent of fallen leaves and distant woodsmoke with it. Above me, the aspen trees shimmered in hues of gold and amber against a backdrop of evergreens and jagged mountain peaks.

The last of the aspen leaves rustled softly in the cool mountain breeze, and I was betting that the first snowfall wasn't far away. Fall might be my favorite season. I only wish I could stop to enjoy it this year, and this murder wasn't hanging over our heads.

"Hi there, is Virginia in today?" I asked the woman at the desk as I rubbed my hands together to warm them.

"She is," she assured me, "but she's in a meeting right now."

"Do you have any idea how long it might be?"

"They should be wrapping up shortly. Would you like to leave a message?"

"I think I'll just hang out for a little bit and wait," I explained.

"As soon as I see her, I'll let her know you're here," she said.

"Wonderful. Thank you!"

While I waited, I browsed the shelf of newly released cookbooks. Not that I had time to cook, but I always wanted to. I could invite Juliet and Wendy over for Thanksgiving dinner this year. Clara would be thrilled. Assuming Juliet wasn't in jail then.

As I perused the shelves, I glanced through the stacks but stopped cold when I saw him. Eliot Thornfield was sitting at a table in the Reference section, surrounded by several large books as he typed on his laptop.

And there you go. I wouldn't have to drive out to the edge of the woods by myself after all. I could just walk across the library and interrogate, er, I mean, introduce myself to him while surrounded by other library patrons.

"Excuse me, Mr. Thornfield," I whispered when I reached his table.

"Yes?" He looked up at me, confusion painted on his features as he adjusted his glasses and tugged on his shirt sleeves.

"I understand you're writing a book on the history of Glenwood?"

"Why yes! As a matter of fact, I am. And you are?"

"I'm Holly Daniel, and I only moved here a few years ago, so I'm fascinated by the history. It's quite colorful."

"Oh, my, yes, colorful is one way to describe it," he said, before tilting his head. "Have we met?"

"I don't think so, but you've probably seen me around. It's a small town, after all. Have you written other books, or is this your first?"

"I'll have you know, I am a best-selling author of several books," he responded, jutting his chin forward. I wanted to ask their titles but I had more important questions first.

"You were a contestant in the pie-baking contest, too, right?"

"Yes," he tsked. "What a tragedy. I can't believe that man died right in front of us."

"What prompted you to enter the competition? Considering you're so new here."

"I think it's important to really get a feel for the Glenwood Springs community while I write this book, and I figured what better way than enter a contest. Besides," he leaned forward to whisper, "it could only help with sales of my future book, don't you think?"

"I imagine it would." I nodded.

"But I also feel like community involvement would add depth to the book. And just between you and me," he winked, "I've always thought of myself as a rather talented amateur chef."

"I guess that makes sense then. What kind of pie did you make?"

"Oh, it was no big deal. I just whipped up a little French Tarte Tatin."

"That sounds fancy!" I exclaimed. "And I don't even know what it is. Is it really a pie?"

"It's not that hard with a little practice. And it's kind of a pie. A tarte for sure, but it's almost the French version of our apple pie."

"It's a shame no one got to try it!" I exclaimed.

He parked his elbows on the table, placed his head in his hands, and stared at me. "I agree!"

"Are you staying at the Red Castle Hotel while you're here?" I asked, not wanting to tip my hand.

"No, I rented the cutest little cottage at the edge of town. The one that backs to the forest."

"Really? All the way out there? Don't you get lonely?" I asked.

"Not at all. I appreciate the peace and quiet while I'm working. But it's another good excuse to get involved with community events. So I'm not just sitting at home all day writing."

"Did you know Sebastian LeClair was new to Glenwood as well?"

"Hey," he laughed. "I'm the one who's supposed to be the writer here. But you're the one asking all the questions. Are you a writer too?"

"Oh, no, not at all."

"Then what *do* you do, Ms. Daniel?"

I hesitated. I was sure he'd clam up like Mabel once I admitted who I was. "Well, I'm a Paranormal Private Investigator."

Eliot blinked rapidly and shifted in his seat before recovering. I really must invent a cover story when I talk to suspects. Private Investigators made *everybody* nervous, whether they were guilty or not!

"You don't say? So, tell me, Ms. Daniel, Private Investigator, why so many questions? Are you investigating LeClair's death? Questioning all the contestants?"

"I'm just curious, that's all."

"I see," he responded before pausing to point to the front desk. "I think the woman at the desk is trying to get your attention."

I swiveled to find the woman I talked to earlier was waving at me. "I'm so sorry. I'll be right back," I told him.

"Is Virginia free now?" I asked.

The woman shook her head. "She's taking longer than she expected in her meeting. Would you like to leave a message?"

"Sure, I can do that. I'd also like to check these out," I told her, handing her the cookbooks I'd selected.

"I can do that for you right over here," she told me, pointing to the checkout desk.

"Thank you, let me just--" I planned to tell Eliot not to leave, but when I turned around, he was gone. Phooey. So much for asking him more about why he chose to write a book about Glenwood Springs and why LeClair was yelling at him in the kitchen.

After the clerk had processed my books and handed me the checkout receipt, I realized it was payday! How could I forget that? I could stop by the hotel on my way home to pick up my check and hopefully do some additional investigating. I feared I was running out of time which meant Juliet was running out of time.

TWELVE
JOIN THE GHOSTS

I parked in the employee lot to pass through the kitchen first, hoping to find someone willing to talk again about what they may have seen before LeClair was murdered. On my way through, I watched for anyone, ghost or living, who looked like they'd be up for a chat, but the talkative ghosts were nowhere to be seen, and the staff were extra busy dealing with an unexpectedly large party in the restaurant so they weren't free to answer questions anyway. Sure, they threw me a quick hello, but they clearly didn't have time to talk at length. Oh well. It's not like it was a wasted trip. It was payday!

I picked up my check and returned to the parking lot, but a fluttering piece of paper on the windshield caught my eye as I approached the bus. At first, I assumed it was an advertising flyer, but none of the other cars had one. Oh no. What if someone ran into it and left a note? I quickened my pace, scanning the bus for any apparent damage, but saw none.

I slid the paper from the windshield wiper, and stopped cold when I read it.

Stop or you'll join the ghosts.

I read it again while my heart raced and my knees shook so badly I had to brace myself against the bus. My gaze darted about the quiet parking lot as I suddenly felt exposed and vulnerable. I spun around twice, thinking I'd somehow spot the perpetrator lurking nearby. But there was no one. Who could have done this? It had to be LeClair's killer, right? And it had to be someone who knew this was my bus, which didn't narrow the list down much. Everyone knew it. The cheerful color of my beautiful VW suddenly seemed garish and attention-grabbing.

My mind raced with possibilities. What if Mabel was following me? Given how rattled she got, the more I questioned her, she could want to scare me off. Which meant I was on the right track. Or what about Eliot? Considering I had just talked to him less than an hour ago, right before he disappeared on me!

I pondered my next move. This was serious, and I had to call Sheriff Mack whether I wanted to or not. I groaned. I could hear the lecture already.

I had to admit, I was a little scared. Someone knew I was getting too close. Someone who had killed already could kill again to keep their secret. I opened the door to check the back seats in case someone was hiding. Although, had they actually been hiding there, I wasn't sure what I'd have done. Run fast, I guess!

As much as I didn't want to involve Sheriff Mack, he had resources that I didn't. Could he check for fingerprints? I glanced back at the hotel, but none of the security cameras were aimed at the employee parking lot. Not this section, anyway. I turned around and around again, scanning nearby buildings for cameras, but I didn't see any. With a heavy sigh, I opened my phone, snapped a picture of the note, then pressed the sheriff's name to call him.

"This better be good," he growled after answering on the first ring.

"Someone left a note on my car when I was in the hotel," I exclaimed.

"A secret admirer?" he grunted.

"No. Not exactly."

"Did someone run into your car?" he asked, turning concerned.

"Nooo."

"Then what is it?" he said, becoming impatient.

After I read the note to him, he cursed softly. "I knew this would happen. Don't move. I'll be right there. No, wait. Go back into the hotel, where there are other people around. You'll be safer there."

"I'm not really that worri--"

"Just do what I say for once. Please!" he barked.

"Okay, okay," I lifted my hand in surrender. "I'll wait for you in the hotel lobby."

"I'm about five minutes out," he reassured me.

"Okay, see you soon."

Why did I have to wait inside? If someone really wanted to hurt me out here, they'd have done it by now, wouldn't they? But I was already steeling myself for the inevitable scolding, and I didn't want to make it worse. I shut the bus door and locked it before trudging back inside.

While I waited in the lobby, Tim, the busser I had talked before, passed by, nodding his head in silent greeting. But then he stopped in his tracks. "Oh! Hi there, Holly!"

"Hi, Tim," I responded, hiding the note behind my back. No need to freak out everyone else.

"Remember when you asked me the other day if I'd seen

anything suspicious in the kitchen before the pie competition started?"

"Yes! Did you remember something?"

"I didn't, but I was talking to Jenny, who was tending bar that day--"

"Jenny, yes, of course!" I snapped my fingers. Why hadn't I thought to ask her? Considering she was there serving us all drinks after LeClair died. "What did she say?"

"She saw Pastor Greg lurking in the kitchen before the judging started."

Good grief. Was everyone in the kitchen, despite being warned it was off limits? However, I still didn't believe anyone who claimed they saw Juliet in there because she said she wasn't. But that made Daisy the only one that wasn't seen in the kitchen. Not yet anyway. "Did she ask him why he was in the kitchen when it was off limits?"

"No, she said she didn't really care that he was there, but it stuck out in her mind when she heard me asking about it."

"Okay, thanks, Tim. I appreciate the update. If you hear anything more, let me know."

"Will do." He nodded.

Several minutes later, while I was still pondering the latest development, the sheriff's SUV screeched to a halt in front of the hotel, where I headed out to greet him. He said nothing but held out his hand for the note. After reading it, he groaned, pinching the bridge of his nose as he often did when he was frustrated.

"Are you okay?" he asked.

"Yes, I'm fine. But thanks for asking." I smiled because I actually meant it.

"Did you see anyone suspicious hanging around the area?"

"Nope." I shook my head.

"Were you in the hotel when it happened?"

"I think so. I didn't notice it before I arrived."

"Why were you here?"

"I was picking up my paycheck, Mr. Nosy Pants."

"Holly, this is important. I have to know everything."

"Fine. First, I was at the library, then I came here to pick up my check."

"Why were you at the library?"

I *hoped* he wouldn't ask that, but I wasn't surprised that he did.

"I was checking out books..." I responded so haltingly it made me cringe. He gave me the look I've come to know all too well.

"Annnd?" he pressed.

"And, I had hoped to talk to Virginia, the librarian, but she was in a meeting."

"Talk to her about what?"

"I heard rumors about Eliot Thornfield, and I wanted to discuss them with her," I responded in almost a whisper, hoping he wouldn't hear me that well.

"So you went to the library to continue investigating the case, even though I told you not to. What did the librarian say?"

"I never got a chance to talk to her. I had to leave a message."

"So that's all you did. Check out books, and leave a message for the librarian."

"Not exactly," I muttered.

"Why is there always more with you?" he scolded, shaking his head.

"Eliot Thornfield was in the library when I got there... But!" I interrupted before he could even ask. "I didn't know that before I arrived. I swear!"

"Did you question him about his involvement in the pie competition?"

"Yes." What else could I say? It was too late to come up with a better story.

"Do you see why I tell you not to get involved? This is dangerous work. Someone murdered Sebastian LeClair--"

"Ah ha!" I shouted. "So you don't think it's Juliet!"

"That's beside the point. *Someone* murdered Sebastian LeClair," he repeated, waving the note in the air, "and yet you insist on snooping around, and now you've angered that someone. Probably the killer. Have you spoken with anyone other than Mabel or Eliot?"

"No, those were the only two. And we don't even know for certain that the note was for me. It could have been for someone else, and they got the wrong car." Even as I said it, I didn't believe it. But I had to offer something to defend myself.

Sheriff Mack ignored the last part. "Even though you've only talked to Mabel and Eliot, anyone could have overhead you, including the killer, who decided it was only a matter of time before you got to them!"

"I guess," I mumbled.

"Please. Go home, and I'll call you if I find out anything about this note. And watch your back," he said, slipping it into an evidence bag.

"All right. All right. I'll go home."

"Promise me!' he demanded.

"I promise you I'll go home." I could add that I had already planned to do that, but I'll be smart about it and not say anything else for once.

On the way home, I mulled over everything I'd learned. Was I really in danger? I didn't think so. However, it couldn't hurt to be cautious.

Sheriff Mack was right. Someone *did* kill Sebastian. But why? What if he knew something the killer didn't want anyone else to know? Would they kill again to keep their secret from getting out? What if Mabel cheated? Or really was lying about the ingredients in her preserves? Did Eliot know something about LeClair that the rest of us didn't? He made a fancy French tart for the competition. What if he knew LeClair from when the Chef lived in France? So many questions, so few answers.

I sighed loudly when I walked into the kitchen, dropping the cookbooks on the kitchen table.

"What did you get?" Clara asked.

"I picked up some cookbooks. I thought we could have Thanksgiving here this year."

"Yes!" Clara exclaimed, clapping her hands while jumping around. "This is so exciting. Oh! I know what we could make! A Jell-O mold!"

"A Jell-O mold?" I asked.

"Yes! They were all the rage in the 1950s."

"Okayyy," I responded, still unsure why the thought of a Jell-O mold was so exciting.

"I think it was 1954 when I made my famous Tuna Jell-O salad. It was fabulous."

"Tuna?" I exclaimed in shock. She was kidding, right? "Mystery, are you okay?" I asked as Mystery heaved like she was spitting up a large hairball.

"Tuna Jello-O salad? That sounds awful," Mystery said.

"How do you know? Have you ever tried it?" Clara responded, annoyed that Mystery would shoot down her suggestion so quickly.

"I think it killed me once," Mystery insisted.

"Oh, it did not!" Clara exclaimed.

"Okay, maybe not," she laughed. "But it sounds like something that could have killed me."

"I'll probably regret asking this, but why a Jell-O mold?" I said.

"Because we enjoyed making molds."

"You liked your dinner molded?"

"Pretty much. Yes." She nodded as if it made perfect sense. "It had lemon gelatin, mayonnaise, onion, cucumber, tuna, olives, celery--"

"Now I know that killed me," Mystery insisted.

"I'm sure there are plenty of dishes we could try that don't involve tuna and Jell-O and won't make Mystery gag every time we mention them," I pointed out.

"Who are we inviting?" Clara asked, ignoring Mystery's dramatics but still excited about a Thanksgiving dinner at the house.

"Wendy and Juliet, of course. Assuming we know who really murdered LeClair by then."

"And Sheriff Mack," Clara added.

"Sheriff Mack? Why would we invite him?"

"Why wouldn't we? He's dreamy," she said, clasping her hands against her chest and getting all gooey-eyed.

"I'm sure he has family somewhere. He's probably going there."

"Still, you should ask him," she insisted.

"Back in my day, we didn't invite the popo to family gatherings," Mystery added, but we ignored her.

"Mmmm, we'll see. He isn't too happy with me as usual, though."

"Why? What did you do?" Clara asked.

"Why do you assume it's my fault?"

"Isn't it always?"

"He's annoyed that I'm neck deep in this investigation,

and he was even more upset when I told him about the threatening note."

"Threatening note! What are you talking about?" Clara exclaimed.

Oh dear, why did I tell her that? Now, she'll worry, too.

"When I was in the hotel picking up my paycheck, someone left a note on my car warning me to stay out of the investigation." I pulled out my phone to show her the picture.

"You need to be more careful," she insisted, her ghostly form flickering with worry. "Whoever left this note clearly knows about your abilities."

"That doesn't narrow it down much. A lot of people are aware of my abilities," I reminded her.

"I think they're watching the house right now," Mystery said from her perch in the window.

"What?" I exclaimed as Clara, and I rushed to the window to see who was out there. I squinted into the dark while my pulse raced at the thought that whoever left the note on my bus knew it was me, knew I could talk to ghosts, and knew where I lived. I clutched my phone tighter as I prepared to call Sheriff Mack.

"Ha! Ha! Made you look!" Mystery chuckled.

"You're lucky you don't have ten lives," I muttered, stomping from the room—the things I had to put up with...

THIRTEEN

A DIFFERENT DAISY

I woke up the following morning and got right back to work. I refused to let a threatening note stop me because Juliet was counting on me. A quick search on the internet told me Daisy Thompson taught cooking classes at the Mountain View Adult Education Center, and lucky for me, today she was teaching a class on pasta making. I couldn't picture how that shy, mousy girl, who was so nervous at the competition that she was on the verge of tears, could stand in front of a group of people and teach them cooking skills, but now was the time to find out.

"Clara, I'm going to the Mountain View Adult Education Center to talk to Daisy Thompson. I'll be back in a little while!" I called out. No Clara. "Clara? Clara?" I asked, wandering through the house. Perhaps she was in the garden reading. But no Mystery either. What were they up to? As soon as I slid into the driver's seat, I learned precisely what they were doing.

"We're going with you!" Clara exclaimed.

"Yikes!" I yelped, clutching my hand to my chest. It had been a while since they got the jump on me like that. I inherited the pink bus because the previous owners had left it behind, which annoyed me in the beginning. (I was annoyed by a lot of things those days.) I had a perfectly fine Subaru that I drove from Florida, thank you very much. Only it wasn't perfectly fine because it died shortly after I arrived.

And while I wasn't exactly broke between my husband's life insurance and severance from my last job, I didn't want to spend a bunch of money on a new car, either. Lo and behold, parked in the garage was a fully restored vintage VW bus just for me.

I couldn't understand why they'd leave a vehicle behind that they'd obviously spent so much time on. But Clara eventually admitted they thought the bus was haunted. Even though most ghosts can't leave the property where they passed, Clara and Mystery can. As long as they were riding in the bus. Perhaps because it was restored on the property where they died? That was my best guess, but who really knew?

You see, one day, while the previous owners were test driving it, Clara discovered something remarkable - she could remain in the bus even as they drove away from the house. The VW bus had somehow become an extension of her haunted domain. Clara was so excited at the discovery she leaped up and threw her feet forward, accidentally kicking the driver's seat and nearly causing him to wreck. They went home and put the house on the market the next day.

I've tried offering rides to other ghosts, thinking it might be a special paranormal vehicle, but it never worked. So Clara and Mystery enjoy riding along and waving at people. It always made me giggle when I wondered what the pedestrians we pass on the sidewalk would think if they knew a

145-year-old ghost and a talking cat were waving at them. Clara has tried to talk me into a horn that plays the theme from Batman. But I kept telling her no. She wanted a cell phone, too, but that wasn't happening.

"We should go to the Sheriff's Department," Clara announced.

"Why? So I can get yelled at for not backing off the investigation?"

"No, so I can see Sheriff Mack. He's such a hunk. Especially in his uniform. Don't you think?"

I rolled my eyes and refused to respond.

"Where *are* we going?" Mystery asked.

"Daisy Thompson is teaching a class at the Adult Education Center this afternoon."

"You think she eighty-sixed the chef?" Mystery asked, making a slashing motion across her throat.

"Maybe. Juliet caught her in a serious discussion with Sebastian LeClair the day before the competition, and Daisy knew he was staying at the Red Castle Hotel. Why would she know something like that? And what were they arguing about? Except, as nervous as she is, I think she'd need her mother's permission to kill someone," I explained half jokingly.

"Her mother would tell her it's okay to kill someone?" Clara asked, aghast.

"Cool!" Mystery exclaimed. "My mama taught me how to kill. Mice, snakes, birds. I've killed plenty of mice in my time. And crickets. Oh, and grasshoppers."

"Thanks for sharing," I told her.

"Grasshoppers are tasty, but man, those sticky legs are a serious hassle. I'd get those darn things stuck in my whiskers, and I wouldn't know it, and then another cat would see the leg dangling from my face and laugh at me.

And sometimes, they still wiggle around while I'm chewing on them. That's weird. They're delightfully crunch--"

"All right, Mystery, we get the picture," I cut her off.

"Could we visit the coffee shop drive-through?" Clara asked.

A drawback of allowing these two to ride along was their constant requests for detours, like the coffee shop. I even had to set up a special cup holder for Clara to drink her frappuccino. And Mystery loved the catppucino - whipped cream in a cup. You can imagine the barista's face when I asked for a cup of whipped cream, only to place it in the empty back seat with a warning not to spill it because I didn't want a sticky mess.

We finally arrived at the Adult Learning Center, where I told Mystery and Clara to stay in the bus. It's funny to me because they can't leave. But they never laughed at that joke. Even though I laughed at plenty of their dumb jokes!

After asking three people where I could find Daisy's cooking class, I eventually located her on the second floor. I snuck into the room and sat in a chair in the corner while her back was turned, writing on the chalkboard. Today's lesson was quick and easy pasta dishes, and the Daisy I saw lecturing in front of the room and guiding students through their problems was most definitely not the Daisy I encountered at the competition. What on earth?

I'm not saying she was ready for the Food Network or anything like that, but she was far more confident and relaxed when talking to this class than she was around her mother. Luckily, I arrived just as it was wrapping up, so I didn't have to wait long to approach her.

"Hello there," she said, surprised to see someone sitting in the back of the room after the rest of the students left.

"Hi! Forgive me for barging in like this, but I saw you at

the pie competition and was hoping to talk to you about it. I'm Holly Daniel, by the way. I'm a Paranormal Private Investigator."

Daisy bristled, immediately shoving a finger in her mouth to chew on. Then, I noticed the dark circles under her eyes, partially hidden behind her thick glasses, that weren't noticeable from the back of the room. It appeared that she was under a lot of stress. The stress of murdering someone? "What do you want to talk about?" she stuttered.

Now, that was more like the Daisy I saw at the competition. But it was also an about-face from Daisy, the teacher. Which one was real? Was it both? Was it an act to hide something?

"I heard you argued with Sebastian LeClair the day before the contest. Can you tell me what that was about?"

Daisy's fingers found a hangnail, and she picked at it nervously. "It was nothing, really. Just... just about the rules. He thought my pie shouldn't be allowed because of a technicality."

I stared at her. "A technicality? What kind of technicality?"

"It's silly," Daisy said, her voice barely above a whisper. She glanced around as if afraid someone might overhear. "He said the decorative details on my chocolate cream pie were too intricate for an amateur baker and that I must have had help."

"Did you?" I pressed gently.

Daisy's fingers moved faster, picking at her already ragged nails. A small bead of blood appeared on her thumb. "Well, yes. I mean, no. I mean... it wasn't fair. I worked so hard on that pie."

"We also have a witness who saw you in the kitchen before the judging started, even though contestants weren't supposed to be there. Can you tell me what you were doing?"

"If you must know, I was trying to get away from my mother!" she cried.

Yikes. I didn't actually have a witness who saw her. I just thought I'd throw it out there to see how she responded.

"Why were you trying to get away from your mother?"

Tears welled up in Daisy's eyes. "I can't... I shouldn't... oh, what would Mother say?" She began to hyperventilate, her eyes darting around wildly. "I have to go. I'm sorry, I can't do this."

Before I could say another word, Daisy turned and fled, leaving me alone in the classroom to digest everything she just told me.

"Were you able to talk to Daisy?" Clara asked when I got in the bus a while later.

"Kind of. But then she took off."

"Where did she go?" Mystery asked.

"Beats me." I shrugged. "I looked for her after she left but couldn't find her anywhere."

"Where to now?" Mystery asked.

"Coffee shop!" Clara exclaimed.

"All right, all right, we'll go to the coffee shop!"

But as I headed toward the nearest coffee shop, I glanced in the rearview mirror only to be surprised by flashing blue and red lights. "What the heck?" I muttered. "Did I run a red light?"

"I don't think so," Clara replied.

"Then why am I being pulled over?"

Mystery and Clara spun around in their seats. "Way to go! You brought the fuzz down on us!" Mystery declared before jumping in the back to hide.

Seriously. What was it with that cat?

I pulled over to the side of the road, hoping they'd fly past on their way to somewhere else, but nope. They were definitely pulling me over. I didn't think I was speeding. At most, just a couple of miles over the speed limit anyway. Hardly worth bothering with.

I waited patiently until the deputy got out of his car. Snails! That was no deputy. It was Sheriff Mack. And as usual, he wasn't happy.

FOURTEEN
QUESTIONS AND CONFESSIONS

"Ms. Daniel." The sheriff nodded as he approached my door.

"Sheriff Mack," I said, nodding back.

"Sheriff Mack! Sheriff Mack!" Clara exclaimed, waving excitedly from the back seat.

"Clara says hello," I told him.

"Hello, Clara," he said to the front seat.

"She's in the back."

"Oh. Sorry. Hello Clara."

"Oh my stars," she sighed before collapsing against the back seat.

"She just pretended to faint," I explained.

"Erm, that's nice. Do you know why I pulled you over?"

"I was speeding?" I asked hopefully.

"No."

"I ran a stop sign, didn't I?"

"No," he sighed. "Why were you at the Adult Education Center?"

"Registering for a class?"

"Which one?"

"Painting! I mean, uh, paint by, uh, paint by numbers?"

He glared at me. "Try again."

"I was teaching a class on, uh, er..."

"How not to lie to law enforcement?" he suggested. "I know you were there questioning Daisy Thompson."

"And how would you know that?"

"Because *I* was there to question Daisy, and wasn't I surprised to find her fleeing the building? When I finally caught up to her and asked her why she was running, she said you were harassing her."

"I was not harassing her!" I insisted. "I was simply curious. I wasn't mean to her if that's what you're thinking."

"Holly--"

Uh oh. I was in trouble now.

"Steve," I responded. Oops. That was dumb.

"For some foolish reason," he started, his mouth tense, "I thought a threatening note would convince you to stay out of this."

"Are you forgetting I'm a private investigator? Licensed even!" I jabbed my finger in the air, reinforcing my point. "And you helped me get that license! Remember?"

"Of course, I remember. But I hoped you would be cautious after what happened yesterday. And not that I want to encourage you, but what did she tell you? Anything useful?"

"I asked her why she was spotted sneaking around the kitchen before the competition."

"How did you know that?" he asked.

"I didn't. I just said it to see how she'd respond, and she admitted to it." I smiled when I caught a look of surprise and perhaps even a tiny bit of admiration. If I didn't know any better, I'd say Sheriff Mack was impressed. "She said she was hiding from her mother, by the way. What did she tell you?" When he hesitated, I pouted. "C'mon. I gave you something, fair is fair. Did she tell you anything good?"

"I shouldn't share this with you, but she told me she saw Pastor Greg getting kicked out of the kitchen area before the competition. But please, please, be careful and let me handle this."

"I promise I'll be careful."

"I'd consider locking you up to keep you safe, but that involves a lot of paperwork I don't feel like doing."

"Have a nice day, Sheriff," I told him as he was about to walk away.

"You can lock me up!" Clara shouted after him.

"Clara!" I scolded. "Control yourself."

"I never could control myself around a lawman," she sighed.

I shook my head as I put the bus in drive and drove away from the curb. I had the strangest roommates.

"Is it clear? Is the popo gone?" Mystery said, peeking out from behind the back seat.

I stand by what I said. Strange.

"Coffee shop drive-through?" Clara reminded me.

She loved to watch me order coffee at the drive-through speaker and refused to let me use the app. But still, the coffee shop would wait for the moment because I just spotted Pastor Greg's church in the distance.

"We'll do the coffee shop after I talk to Pastor Greg," I told them, pulling into the church parking lot.

"Is that the guy on TV?" Mystery asked.

"TV?"

"Yeah, he's on TV on Sunday mornings. *Get saved with Pastor Greg*," Mystery sang off tune.

"He's very pretty," Clara pointed out.

"Yes, I noticed at the competition. I think he wears more makeup than I do."

"He's like one of those Hollywood types, with the hair and the long eyelashes. Personally, I prefer a real man. Like Sheriff Mack."

"Yes, Clara, we know."

As I navigated into a parking spot near the front door, I admired the little white church nestled against the mountainside, its steeple reaching tall into the crisp Colorado sky. Concrete steps led up to the front doors, flanked by flowering mountain paintbrush and columbine that were fading out for the winter yet continued to add the last splashes of red and purple to the simple exterior. Jewel toned stained glass windows greeted all who entered while a wooden sign read: Mountain View Chapel, Pastor Greg Fletchen.

Inside was the familiar scent of wood polish and old hymnals, while a center aisle led between several rows of wooden pews to a raised pulpit at the front. In the back of the sanctuary was a small audio-visual setup - evidence of Pastor Greg's local television broadcasts. The modern equipment looked somewhat out of place among the church's otherwise humble furnishings.

"Good afternoon! How can I help you?" a man in a t-shirt that read *Pastor*, who I immediately recognized as Pastor Greg from the pie baking competition, asked me.

Fortunately, he didn't seem to recognize me from the hotel bar when we talked after LeClair's murder. Clara was right. He was very pretty.

Wendy mentioned how he often came into the store looking for books on theology, but she noticed he liked to hang around and ask her and other customers about certain townspeople. She said it was almost like he was purposefully looking for gossip.

"Hi there! I'm Holly Daniel, and I'm a Paranormal Private Investigator. Could I ask you some questions about the pie competition you were just in?"

"Private Investigator? Are you working with the Sheriff's Department?"

"Not exactly..." I trailed off.

"You're in a church. You probably shouldn't lie, you know," he said with a gleam in his eye.

"For this case, no. I'm investigating on my own."

"Fair enough. What would you like to know, Holly?"

"Why *did* you enter the competition?"

"You ask that like you don't see how a man of the cloth can be a pie baker."

"No, not at all. I'm always curious about why people do certain things. You seem awfully busy. You run a church and you're on TV and all over social media. How did you find the time to enter a pie baking competition?"

"I think it's important to get involved and promote community spirit."

"That makes sense. And you aren't the first person to tell me that. What kind of pie did you make?"

"Uhhh, blueberry."

"You sound unsure."

"I changed my mind a couple of times before deciding on blueberry."

"I see. And can you tell me why you were in the kitchen before the judging began? Even though it was off limits?"

"Who told you that?"

"So you don't deny it?"

"You still haven't admitted where you got that information."

"I heard you had to be escorted from the kitchen."

"Okay, you got me. I needed a drink of water but didn't

want to bother the staff because they were busy with the competition."

"By the way, do you happen to know what kind of vehicle I drive?"

"You have that bright pink bus, right? Everyone knows that."

I nodded. He was right. Everyone knew. Which meant anyone could have placed the note on my bus. "When was the last time you were at the Red Castle Hotel?"

"The hotel? I haven't been to the hotel since the competition. What are you getting at here?"

"I'm only trying to put an accurate timeline together. But I--" His phone chimed Before I could finish my thought.

"Sorry about that," he said. "That's my reminder that I have to visit a parishioner who's in the hospital after having surgery, so I must go. Sorry I couldn't be more helpful. But you should stop in for a service sometime."

"Yes, that would be nice," I told him.

When I returned to the bus, Mystery and Clara peppered me with questions I couldn't really answer. "I don't trust that guy."

"Why?" Clara asked.

I shrugged. "Just a hunch, I suppose."

I glanced at my phone when it dinged with a text. It was Gerald from the hotel.

> Holly, Teresa called out sick tonight. Can you sub?

Perfect timing. That way, I had a built-in excuse to be at the hotel, and if I happened to discover clues while I was bartending, then technically, that didn't count as investigating. That was my story anyway, and I was sticking to it.

"I have to work tonight, guys. Do you want me to drop you off at home, or do you want to come with?"

"You promised us a trip to the coffee shop!" Mystery scowled at me from the back seat.

"Yes! Coffee shop!" Clara cheered.

"All right, all right, coffee shop it is."

"And then you can drop us off at home because *Charlie Brown Thanksgiving* is on TV tonight," Mystery reminded me.

At the drive-through speaker, I ordered an espresso for myself (it might be a late night after all), a London Fog tea latte for Clara, and a catppucino for Mystery.

After the barista handed me the drinks, I carefully placed Clara's in her special cupholder before putting Mystery's catppucino in the back seat. "Nobody spill anything, got it? Remember, I just cleaned in here and don't have time to do it again right away."

When I saw the barista staring at me I responded with a shake of my head. "Ghosts. What are you going to do?"

FIFTEEN

SHADOWS OF THE PAST

I was in the laundry area picking out a clean waist apron when Charles appeared. "Psst! Hey, breather!"

"Charles! Good evening! What's up?"

"LeClair hid something in his hotel room that the cops haven't found."

"Hid something? What is it?" I asked skeptically. I doubted the Sheriff's Department would miss anything.

"LeClair put something in an envelope and hid it in the vent."

When I stared back at Charles without responding, he had a flair for the dramatic after all, he scowled and threw up his hands. "You're the one investigating the guy's death, and I just now remembered him doing that. I don't care how this goes either way, and I was only trying to be helpful."

"Okay, okay, don't get grumpy," I reassured him. "You're right. I asked you to be my eyes and ears. But what can I do about it? Aside from letting the sheriff know?"

"You could get the master key and sneak in there..." Charles suggested with a glint in his eye.

Was he trying to get me in trouble on purpose? Ghost

life could be dull, and they often enjoyed stirring up chaos. But what if he wasn't? What if he was telling the truth? That LeClair had hidden something so well that the investigation hadn't uncovered it?

Of course, I should tell Sheriff Mack. But he might refuse to share what he found. And if I took just a teensy peek first, I'd learn what was in it. What if it was a secret recipe like the others had suggested? Maybe it even named his killer without meaning to? I should do this, right? My best friend was still a murder suspect, while the real killer was free to wander about town. I glanced at my watch and realized I still had a few minutes before my shift started.

"Make it quick!" I told Charles, who was delighted by the decision. I snuck into the office and grabbed the master key, with Charles following my every step. The hotel had security cameras, but they often quit without warning, so I hoped this was one of those times.

"Which vent?" I asked him once we got into the room.

"That one," he said, pointing at a spot on the floor near the bed.

I bent down and pried off the vent cover. Charles was right! There was an envelope taped to the duct. I carefully removed it, then slowly lifted the flap as if something might jump out at me. I hoped my hands weren't too sweaty and I wasn't leaving fingerprints all over it. I vowed to glance at the contents, then put it right back. After that, I could text Sheriff Mack and tell him what Charles had witnessed. No harm, no foul, right?

The first thing I pulled out of the envelope was a small, somewhat grainy picture of three grinning young boys with their arms around each other. Maybe pre-teens? I turned it over, but the back was blank. Okay, that didn't tell me much. In addition to the photo was a piece of folded paper. Maybe this was the secret recipe!

I KNOW WHO YOU ARE

I yelped out loud when I read it, then pressed my hand against my mouth. Not only was it most definitely not a recipe, but the handwriting matched the note that was on my bus! My fingers trembled while my legs went weak, and I sank onto the edge of the bed. It was as if I'd been punched in the stomach. But before I could decide what to do next, the doorknob rattled.

"Someone's coming! Hide!" Charles hissed at me before he disappeared. Why did he disappear? It's not like anyone else could see him. I leaped to my feet, spinning in circles in a panic before shoving everything in my apron pocket.

"The bathroom!" Charles whispered from beyond.

"Thanks!" I whispered back while darting into the bathroom, where I crouched behind the door, peeking through the small opening. I just knew it was Sheriff Mack. And what would he say when he found me hiding? I was so going to jail for this. I don't care how much paperwork he had to do.

If it was a deputy who didn't know me, could I get away with pretending to be a maid? But why would I be cleaning a dead man's room? Clara would freak when I didn't come home.

I desperately tried to see who it was, but the narrow opening behind the door wasn't helping. I was certain they would hear my ragged breathing and racing heartbeat.

Why did I do this to myself? Why did I listen to Charles? I could have just told Sheriff Mack he needed to look in the vent in the room, but oh, no, I had to check it out first.

Whoever it was finally moved into view. That was no Sheriff Mack. It wasn't even a deputy. It was a young woman. Holy smokes, was that... Could it be... It was Daisy! What on earth?

She moved cautiously around the room, peering into the vent I forgot to re-cover. Rats! How careless could I be? I saw the key in Daisy's hands was marked MAID in big red letters. She stole a key from the maid! Did she know about the hidden envelope? She could easily have written the note I found. What if she put the note on my bus? And now I was trapped here with a killer, and no one knew except for Charles. This was definitely worse than going to jail. I scanned the bathroom for a weapon, but it was empty. What should I do?

But Daisy moved on from the vent and out of my line of sight again. What was she doing? This was excruciating! Several seconds later, she moved into view again and opened a desk drawer, which she rifled through before pulling out a narrow slip of paper. She stared at it, sighed with relief, stuck it in her pocket, and hurried out the door, leaving me bewildered. What did she take, and how did she know it was there?

Once I was sure she was gone, I rushed to the desk, pulled open the drawer, and searched it. All I saw were takeout menus and some invoices from the hotel that were marked PAID. What the heck?

Before I could decide what to do next, I remembered that I was supposed to be working! The investigation would have to wait. I hurried to the door, cracking it open to make sure Daisy or anyone else wasn't lying in wait. I squeezed out, scrambled to the office to return the master key, and headed for the bar, my mind racing with everything that had just happened. How could I concentrate on work at a time like this?

It wasn't until I got to the bar that I remembered the picture and note were still in my apron pocket. What was wrong with me? Now, I'd have to wait until after my shift to return them.

"How's it going?" I asked Sam, who was wiping down the bar, no doubt waiting for me to take over. "Sorry, I'm a little late. I got distracted," I told him, which was the understatement of the century!

"Eh," he lifted a shoulder, "pretty quiet evening so far. Mostly that guy at the end," he explained, nodding in the direction of a man nursing a drink with melting ice cubes.

"Is he a guest?"

"No, he told me he was at one of the hotels on the other side of the bridge and walked over."

"Cool. As long as I don't have to take away his car keys." I hated having to take someone's keys. Boy, did they get grumpy. Better than the alternative, but it was always a relief when they weren't driving.

"Barkeep!" the man called out, raising his glass.

"What can I do for you?" I asked.

"Can I get anudda scotch on da rocks?" he asked with a thick accent.

"Certainly," I told him. I could tell he already had too much to drink, so I added extra water and ice to his glass, and so I didn't feel too bad about it, I charged him less than usual.

"So, what brings you to town?" I asked.

"Lenny!" he responded, shaking his head sadly.

"Lenny?" I pressed when he said nothing more as if he

had expected me to automatically know who this Lenny person was.

"Me and Lenny go way back together. We're from Brooklyn, you see."

"You're here visiting Lenny?"

"No, he died!" he exclaimed.

"Oh, I'm so sorry."

"I came ta town ta pay my respects."

"That was nice of you to show up. Lenny must been a good friend."

"Da best. Lemme tell ya about the time we broke into Mrs. Fiore's bakery for cannolis. We was about, what, twelve? Thirteen? It was a Tuesday night, and we got this wicked craving for those cannolis. Only problem? Her bakery was closed on Tuesdays.

"But back in those days, she left da back door to da bakery unlocked. Everybody did. So, Lenny gets this bright idea. He says, 'Vinnie, we're goin' in.' Next ting I knows, we was sneakin' in the back door of the bakery.

"We was like two kids in a candy store, stuffing our faces with cannolis, not a care in the world. Then, wouldn't ya know it, we hear sirens. Someone saw us and called da cops. We was trapped, cannoli cream all over our faces, looking like a couple of guilty puppies when Mrs. Fiore shows up with the police.

"Now, here's where Lenny's silver tongue comes in. He looks at Mrs. Fiore, all teary-eyed, and spins this wild tale about how we was actually protecting her bakery from rats. Said we saw one sneaking in and couldn't bear the thought of her beautiful cannolis being ruined. I don't know if she actually bought that story, or if she just felt sorry for us, but in the end, she decides not tah press charges.

"I'm standing dere, jaw on the floor, wondering how we's

got away with it. She even gave us a box of cannolis to take home! I tell ya dat Lenny, he always knew how to talk his way outta anything. Could sell ice to an Eskimo, dat one."

I was curious how much of this story was made up by a man with too much to drink and how much was accurate but I nodded my head and listened along like any good bartender should.

"What's your name by the way?" I asked him.

"Vincent," he responded.

"I'm Holly."

"Speaking of names, you musta met Lenny while he was here?" Vincent asked.

"I don't think so. But I only fill in at the bar occasionally, so the regular staff probably met him," I responded.

"But you obviously knew who he was. Him bein' a celebrity and all."

"Celebrity?" I asked.

"Oh! Sorry. You musta known him by his celebrity name," he explained, using jazz hands and pausing dramatically. "Sebastian LeClair."

SIXTEEN

UNRAVELING THE FACADE

I was so stunned at first I couldn't think of a response. I stared at Vincent, my mouth agape. "What?" was all I could think of.

"Sebastian LeClair was my childhood friend, but he was Lenny back then."

"That can't be true," I said, shaking my head in disbelief.

Vincent let out a dry chuckle and sighed. "Sebastian LeClair," he repeated, his Brooklyn accent thick with amusement. "Y'know, that still cracks me up. To me, he'll always be Lenny from da group home on 83rd Street."

"Group home? Like in foster care?"

"Yeah, we met when we was about, oh, nine or ten? Two scrappy kids with more attitude than sense," Vincent said, a fond smile playing on his lips. "Lenny, he always had big dreams, y'know? Always talking about how he was gonna make it big, be somebody important."

"But, but, he's a French chef," I stammered.

Vincent really laughed then. "Oh man, when I foist saw him on TV wit' that fancy accent and all dat talk about classic French cuisine, I nearly fell off my chair laughin'.

But ya know what? It was so typically Lenny. That kid could barely boil water back in da day, but he always had a knack for reinventin' himself."

"But he went to culinary school! Le Cordon Bleu." I refused to believe it was all an act. I met the guy. Kind of, anyway. That had to be real, right?

"Fuggedaboutit! I'm tellin' you, I know da truth 'bout Lenny. One day he just takes off witout warning, right? Stows away on dis cargo ship headed overseas, but - ya know how Lenny's luck goes - he gets caught. So there he is, figurin' they's gonna throw him ovahboard or somethin', and whaddya know? He talks his way outta it by tellin' 'em he's some sorta cook."

"I take it he was no cook. Not at the time, anyway."

"He just makin' it up as he goes along, right? And whaddya know - turns out da kid could actually cook, at least good enough for dose guys on a ship. So anyway, they dock in France and he splits. Then - get dis - he gets caught stealin' food from dis hoity-toity French place, but Lenny bein' Lenny, he sweet talks the owner into givin' him a job washin' dishes and a place ta crash in da back. I'm tellin' ya, that kid could talk his way outta anything!"

So, if what Vincent told me was true, Sebastian LeClair was a con artist, and we already knew he was a jerk, which could mean the list of people who would like to see him dead extended far beyond just the pie baking contestants. I couldn't decide if that made me happy or not.

It could help me persuade the Sheriff's Department to look beyond Juliet. But it also meant the suspect list could be so long we'd never solve the mystery or fully exonerate Juliet. This had to be the wildest story I'd ever heard. It just couldn't be accurate. "So you're telling me he's self-trained?"

"He ain't never went to none of them fancy schools if

that's whatcha askin'. But I'll tell ya what he did do - he learned from some of them big shot chefs. See, when Lenny wanted somethin', dat was it, he was all in, know what I mean? We stayed in touch, on and off, and I'd get these letters from him, always from some new fancy place. Then one day, he shows up back in the States wit dis made-up resume, and French accent, talks his way into one of them ritzy joints in Manhattan. Before ya know it - boom! - he's got his own restaurant and he's on TV and everythin'. Dat's our Lenny, I'm tellin' ya. Always landin' on his feet," he said, shaking his head but with a flicker of something added—guilt? regret? jealousy?—in his eyes. But it passed so quickly that I decided I might have imagined it.

"Have you lived in Brooklyn this whole time?" I asked.

Vincent shook his head. "Da minute Lenny disappeared, I hightailed it to Canada. Lemme tell ya somethin' - I liked it up dere so much, I stayed for I dunno how many years."

"Did Lenny tell you why he moved to Glenwood Springs?"

"He called me recently, right? Says he's gotta get away from everythin', which I'm tellin' ya, dat don't sound like Lenny at all. Then boom," he clapped his hands so suddenly I jumped, "next thing I know, he's dead. Just like dat."

"If what you're saying is true - that Sebastian LeClair really is this Lenny person..." I started while Vincent nodded vigorously, "I've been thinking the same thing. I mean about him moving here anyway. It didn't make sense that a celebrity who clearly enjoyed his life as a chef and a reality TV star would quit without notice and retire."

Vincent kept nodding. "Ya hit da nail on da head. It wasn't like him at all. I mean, just last summer he's braggin' about how much dough he's got, right? Tellin' me he's gonna buy some ritzy joint out in the Hamptons. Then outta nowhere, he's sick of the whole celebrity thing and quits? Nah, somethin' ain't right there, I'm tellin' ya. He sends me this message about how he's movin' to Colorado, goes on and on about this beautiful little town, says I should come visit. But hey -gettin' murdered? Dat wasn't part of the plan, know what I mean?"

When I thought about what was in my pocket, I told myself I was ridiculous for even considering it... Dare I? I was carrying ill gotten evidence around in my apron, and now I was thinking about showing it to a drunk stranger? Had I completely lost it? For all I knew, this guy was telling the truth about knowing LeClair as a child, but he was the killer.

Sure, it sounded wild, but I was pretty sure I'd seen crazier. But still... What if he could identify the boys in the picture? What if he recognized the handwriting on the note? Maybe LeClair told him about the note? The only way I'd know for certain was if I asked...

"Since you knew Sebastian, uh, Lenny, as a child, is there any way you know who's in this photo?" I asked while carefully sliding it from my apron and placing it in front of him.

Vincent dug a pair of glasses from his shirt pocket and carefully studied the picture. "Well, whadya know? That's me, Lenny, and our friend James. We was all in da same foster home," he said with what I thought was a hint of wistfulness that I saw earlier, or was it something more?

"Did you keep in touch with James too?" I asked, thinking James might be able to fill in more blanks than Vincent did.

"No," he said sadly. "He passed away a long time ago."
"Oh. Well, that's too bad."

"Yeah."

I realized I could regret my next move, but if I had gone this far, I might as well go all in. "Do you know anything about this?" I asked, unfolding the note and placing it next to the picture in front of him.

I remained silent as I studied Vincent's face. Confusion flickered across his features, and I couldn't tell if he genuinely didn't recognize what I was showing him or if he was buying time to craft his response.

"Miss! Excuse me, miss! I broke my wine glass!" a customer called from the other side of the bar. Any other night, I'd have smiled and told her not to worry - broken glasses were just part of the job. But the blood trickling down her hand changed everything.

"Oh dear. I'll be right back!" I told Vincent. "Don't go anywhere. I want to hear more about Seb... I mean Lenny."

"I ain't leavin'!" Vincent said, raising his glass of whiskey.

I hurried over to examine the customer's hand, relieved to discover the cut was superficial. Though it was bleeding, it wasn't deep enough to need stitches. "Come on," I said, gently helping her to her feet. "The front desk has a first aid kit and a nurse on call. We'll get this cleaned up and bandaged - it's just a minor cut, nothing to worry about."

After escorting her to the front desk, where they promised to call the nurse to examine her hand, I hurried back to the bar to continue my conversation with Vincent...

Who wasn't there...

Oh no! Where did he go? Please tell me he was in the bathroom. Or outside smoking. Please tell me he'd be right back. I had so many more questions.

But all that remained at his spot were an empty whiskey glass and a handful of crumpled bills - he'd vanished without a word, taking his, *and my,* secrets with him.

SEVENTEEN
LOST AND FOUND

"No, no, no, no!" I whispered furiously, my heart hammering in my chest when I realized what was missing. The photograph and the note were gone - evidence that could break this whole case wide open had vanished along with a stranger who claimed his name was Vincent.

I dropped to my knees, desperately searching under the bar stools, my hands shaking as I patted the floor. Maybe he'd accidentally knocked them to the floor on the other side, I told myself. I popped back up, scanning the bar top, before hurrying over to check the floor there. Nothing. I moved the empty whiskey glass and lifted the scattered bills as if he could hide the picture and note under them while my panic spiked.

Deep down, I knew the truth. Vincent, or whoever he was, took them deliberately. But why? What was in the photo, in the note, that was worth stealing? As I stood there, surrounded by oblivious bar patrons, a cold realization settled in my gut - he could know more about Sebastian's murder than he was letting on, and I'd just handed him the only proof I had that might clear Juliet.

Now, all I had was a story about some guy who supposedly knew Sebastian LeClair when they were kids. What if he was lying? It sounded almost too fantastical, and yet, I tended to believe him. But what would I tell Sheriff Mack? That I accidentally, on purpose, stole evidence from the victim's hotel room? And turned it over to a stranger? How did I get myself into these messes?

In desperation, I fell to my hands and knees one more time, frantically scanning the floor again.

"Holly?"

The familiar voice from above stopped me short. Sheriff Mack! My mind raced with panic - he knew about the break-in, the stolen evidence, everything. I was about to be arrested in front of a bar full of people!

I popped up as casually as I could manage, brushing imaginary dirt from my pants while trying to slow my hammering heart. "Oh, hey!"

"What were you doing down there?" His eyes narrowed slightly.

"Lost something," I said, aiming for nonchalance but landing somewhere closer to suspicious. "Just a... thing. You know how it goes."

"Right..." He raised his eyebrows.

Great job, Holly. Way to act completely guilty for no reason.

"Actually, I have some news for you," he said.

"I didn't mean to take them!" The words burst out before I could stop them.

His brow furrowed. "Take what?"

My cheeks burned as I realized my mistake. He didn't know anything. Of course, he didn't. I was practically confessing to a crime he hadn't even discovered yet.

"Nothing! Never mind." I forced a bright smile. "What's your news? Did you find the killer?"

"Are you sure you're all right?" he asked. "You're acting kind of weird. Weirder than usual, I mean."

"I'm fine," I insisted.

"Okay, well, the lab results came back. All the pies contained wolfsbane, not just Juliet's."

Relief flooded through me. "That's great! I mean, not great that they were all poisoned, and... what about that package delivered to the bakery? Any evidence there?" What if the package had fingerprints or DNA? What if they were this close to zeroing in on the killer and I didn't have to worry about what I'd found in Sebastian's room? I'd have panicked for nothing.

His head shake deflated my rising hopes. "Nothing. No fingerprints, no traces. Whoever did this was careful."

"But this clears Juliet, right? Not that I ever thought she did it. Obviously. And I know you didn't either..." The words tumbled out in a nervous rush.

"H," his voice had taken on that tone - the one that meant I was acting suspicious again. "Is there something you want to tell me?"

"No! Why would there be?" My voice jumped an octave.

"Juliet isn't cleared. It just means the other contestants are also likely suspects."

"Oh. Okay. Well, better than being the sole suspect, I suppose. But I do have to tell you something," I finally admitted. "A man was here earlier. Said his name was Vincent."

"And?"

"And he claimed to know Sebastian LeClair."

"There's a point to this, right?"

"A big point. He told me that Sebastian LeClair was actually a guy named Lenny from Brooklyn who faked his entire resume."

When Sheriff Mack burst out laughing, I scowled at him.

"I'm serious!" I protested, annoyed that he just laughed at me after I'd worked up the courage to tell him about Vincent.

"I'm sure you are, but this mysterious bar patron's story sounds a bit far-fetched."

"He could be a suspect! He's staying at a hotel across the bridge..."

"Well, that narrows it down," he smirked.

"He told me he came to pay his respects when he heard about the murder." Even as I said it, I realized how weak it sounded without mentioning the evidence Vincent had stolen - evidence I'd obtained illegally.

I desperately wanted to tell Sheriff Mack about the matching threatening notes, about my suspicions that Vincent could be the killer, that I might be next. But confessing meant admitting to breaking into Sebastian's room, and that would definitely get me cut off from the investigation.

"How about this? If you see this Vincent guy again, let me know. I'll question him myself."

"Of course," I agreed quickly.

He studied me thoughtfully. "Are you absolutely sure there isn't anything else you want to tell me?"

Oh, I was sure all right. Sure that I was in way over my head and that somewhere out there, a stranger had evidence I'd stolen - evidence that could solve this whole case. Or get me killed.

"Nope," I lied, forcing a smile. "Nothing at all."

EIGHTEEN

CONFESSIONS & CONSEQUENCES

The second my shift was over, I texted Juliet and Wendy.

Me: Ladies. Meet me at my house in 10 minutes. I have a LOT to tell you.

Wendy: It's a little late isn't it? I'm already in my pajamas...

Me: Come in your pajamas.

Juliet: If this is about the pies I already heard about it. I'm glad they discovered that but still...

Wendy: What about the pies.

Me: The pies are the least of it.

Wendy: WHAT ABOUT THE PIES?

Me: Just meet me at the house.

Ten minutes later, we were all settled in my living room - Wendy and Juliet on the couch, Clara hovering excitedly nearby (she loved company, even though I repeatedly forgot to relay her comments), and Mystery perched on the back of a chair, her tail twitching impatiently.

"Someone better tell me about the pies before I explode," Wendy demanded, leaning on her knees and giving us the death stare.

Juliet took a deep breath. "The lab results came back. All of the pies contained wolfsbane."

"So you're off the hook?" Wendy's eyes lit up.

"That's wonderful!" Clara exclaimed, applauding excitedly.

"Not exactly," Juliet grimaced. "I'm no longer the primary suspect. Now *all* the contestants are under investigation."

Wendy slumped back against the couch. "Please tell me that's not your big news. I mean, I'm happy for you, sweetie," she added quickly to Juliet, "but I was all curled up with the cats, wine in hand, about to start Agatha Christie's *Hallowe'en Party* when you texted, Holls."

"Oh, that's a marvelous one!" Clara chimed in.

"Clara liked that one," I told Wendy.

"I'm eager to start on it," Wendy said, looking opposite from where Clara was hovering.

"She's over there," I pointed with my head.

"Oh, sorry." Wendy smiled in that direction.

"It's quite all right, dear. Do you have *A Holiday for Murder* at the store?"

"Clara wants to know if you have *A Holiday for Murder*."

"I do! I'll have Holly bring it home for you."

"Splendid! Thank you so much," Clara exclaimed.

"Blah blah blah," Mystery complained, her long tail swishing in annoyance. "This was supposed to be exciting."

"You're finally dating the sheriff!" Wendy squealed.

"Finally!" Clara echoed.

"What? No! This is serious, you guys!"

Juliet fixed me with her stern maternal gaze. "Does this involve you taking risks that will upset me?"

I waggled my hand noncommittally. "Ehhh..."

"I should have known," she sighed, shaking her head.

"You already know what we've learned about Mabel, so I don't need to remind you of that," I said as I squirmed under their combined stares.

"Are you about to tell me you went to Eliot's place alone?" Juliet asked.

"No," I said.

"Okay, good."

"I went straight to the library as you suggested."

"And what did Virginia say?" she asked.

"She was in a meeting, so I didn't have a chance to talk to her, but Eliot Thornfield was there working."

"And you confronted him?" Wendy asked. "Did you ask him why we can't find his books anywhere?"

"We had a *conversation*," I corrected her.

"And?" She prompted, staring at me even more intently.

"I asked him about his books, and he still insisted he was a best-selling author, but I held off on pressing him about it to ask why he entered the pie competition in the first place."

"And?" Wendy asked again, getting more impatient by the moment.

"He said he wanted to get involved with the community because it would help him sell more books."

"Did he ask why you wanted to know these things?" Juliet pressed.

"He sure did," I responded.

"Did you tell him you're a private investigator?"

"I did. And then he got all nervous."

Wendy nodded. "You can't blame him for that. I probably would, too, whether I had anything to be guilty about or not," she pointed out. "Then what happened?"

"The woman at the checkout desk called me over. She said Virginia's meeting ran longer than she expected, and I should leave a message. I told Thornfield to wait for me, but when I turned around again, he disappeared."

"But you said you had a lot to tell us," Juliet reminded me.

"Yes," I nodded. "I'm getting there," I insisted while Mystery rolled her eyes from boredom. Why must she be so dramatic? "Then I went to the hotel to pick up my paycheck, but when I left, I found a note on my bus."

"A secret admirer?" Wendy asked.

"No. Not really," I added, picking at the hem of my shirt to stall for time. They wouldn't like what I was about to tell them.

"What do you mean not really?" Juliet asked, scowling at me.

"It was this," I said, showing them the picture I took on my phone.

"Holly!" Juliet scolded. "Why didn't you tell us this before?"

"I haven't had the chance?"

"You must tell Sheriff Mack about this right now!" she demanded.

"Actually, you'll be pleased to know that I called him from the hotel right away, and he rushed over."

"That's good!" Wendy said with surprise.

"While I waited for him to arrive, one of the bussers said

that Jenny, the bartender, told him that she saw Pastor Greg in the kitchen before the competition."

"Was everyone except me in that kitchen?" Juliet asked.

"That's exactly what I thought!" I exclaimed. "For pies that were supposed to be secure, there was a lot of unauthorized traffic moving through there."

"Let's get back to that in a moment. I have a sneaking suspicion I know where this is going, and I won't like it, but what did Sheriff Mack say when he saw the note from your bus?" Juliet asked.

"He told me to stay out of the investigation."

"Which I'm sure you took to heart," she said, rolling her eyes.

"I discovered that Daisy teaches cooking at the Adult Learning Center," I told them, ignoring Juliet's comment.

"And you went to see her!" Juliet exclaimed, throwing her hands up in exasperation.

"I sure did."

"And?" Wendy asked. She was used to Juliet being worried about me, but as I repeated my story out loud, it sounded a lot worse than it felt when I was actually doing it.

"I told her there was a witness who saw her arguing with LeClair before the competition, and I wanted to know what it was about." They waited breathlessly to see how I responded. They may argue that I behaved recklessly, but they still wanted to know what I discovered. "She claimed LeClair told her that her pie was too sophisticated, and he thought she had help."

"Did she?" Wendy asked.

"She gave me a wishy-washy answer and insisted she worked really hard on it. And then she ran away."

"You seem to have that effect on people. You need to work on a cover story," Wendy suggested.

I nodded. "Yes, I was thinking the same thing. But that's not all I discovered about Daisy. And you won't like the next part."

Juliet responded to that by crossing her arms over her chest and slumping against the back of the chair. She knew me too well.

"You've been busy!" Wendy pointed out.

"I have. This is important after all," I said, staring pointedly at Juliet. "Charles, one of the hotel spirits, told me that Sebastian LeClair hid something in his hotel room that the Sheriff's Department hadn't discovered."

"Uh oh," Wendy murmured.

"Please tell me you called Sheriff Mack right away for that, too," Juliet begged hopefully, knowing full well I didn't.

"I hadn't planned to lose the evidence!" I blurted out.

"What do you mean you lost evidence? How did you lose evidence? And why do I feel like you just skipped a big part of the story?" Juliet responded with a scowl.

"I'm getting there. Just give me time!" I shifted uncomfortably in my seat.

"I let myself into Sebastian LeClair's hotel ro--"

"You mean you broke into a crime scene!" Juliet shrieked.

"Whatever you want to call it, that's not what's important," I insisted. "Just give me a chance to finish. Charles pointed out that LeClair hid something in the floor vent, and when I opened it, I found an envelope taped to the side of the air duct. Inside was a picture of three boys and a note that read 'I know who you are,' which matched the handwriting on the note I found on my bus."

"Someone was threatening LeClair!" Juliet exclaimed, practically leaping from her seat, but I raised my hand to ward off her lecture. I needed to finish the story before I lost my confidence.

"I had every intention of telling Sheriff Mack where he could find the evidence, but I was unexpectedly interrupted..." I trailed off for a moment...

"...by Daisy."

"Daisy!" Clara exclaimed while I nodded.

"I hid in the bathroom while Daisy broke into the room, went through the desk, and stole something!"

"Did you confront her?" Juliet asked.

"No, I stayed hidden until she left. Then I realized I was late for work, so I left the room, too."

"What did Sheriff Mack say when you told him where to find the evidence?"

"I didn't tell him. When I got distracted by Daisy, I stuffed it in my apron pocket and kind of forgot it was there." The admission spilled out of me, and what had seemed like a reasonable excuse at the time, now sounded no better than what Daisy had done.

"Holly Marie Daniel!" Juliet snapped, her East Texas accent thick with frustration. "It's bad enough you broke into a dead man's hotel room, but you stole evidence? Evidence in a case where I'm a suspect! What in tarnation were you thinking?"

"My middle name isn't Marie," I told her foolishly.

"That's what you took from that?" her shriek so high pitched that Mystery flattened her ears, leaped from the couch, and ran from the room.

"All right, not important," I admitted. "But believe it or not, I have more to tell you."

"This had better be good," Juliet growled.

If she thought she was mad now, wait until she learned the evidence was missing. I felt worse and worse. What I thought started with helping my friend ended with my losing evidence that might clear her name.

I didn't know *how* it would clear her, but I was sure it was important. Why else would LeClair have hidden it so well? I almost didn't want to admit the rest, she was so angry, but I'd come this far, I had to finish.

"I swear to you, I had every intention of returning the evidence and telling Sheriff Mack where to find it."

"And?" Wendy asked warily while Juliet continued staring at me, steam practically coming from her ears.

"I met this guy named Vincent at the bar," I explained, plowing ahead with the story, which almost sounded like I had an imaginary friend. When I got to the part about the woman breaking the wine glass, an uncomfortable silence hung in the air.

"I'm confused," Juliet said. "You still haven't told us what happened to the picture and the threatening note."

I swallowed hard. I couldn't believe I had to admit it out loud. "Vincent stole it."

NINETEEN
FRIENDS AND FORGIVENESS

"I need some fresh air before I say something improper," Juliet claimed. "No, I want to be alone for a moment," she insisted when Wendy and I stood up to follow her.

"Should I...?" Clara pointed at Juliet after she stomped off, the screen door slamming behind her.

I nodded while Clara followed her.

"Just give her some space," Wendy urged. "In the meantime, tell me more about this Vincent person. Did he really claim that LeClair made everything up? And what was Daisy doing in his room? Do you think she killed him?"

"As for Vincent," I said, wringing my hands with worry. What if I screwed up so badly this time Juliet never spoke to me again? I couldn't bear the thought. "He swears LeClair's background was a complete fabrication. But he had a Michelin Star rated restaurant in New York, so he clearly was a first rate chef. Just without the formal education."

"Holy crepes," Wendy muttered. "Talk about fake it 'til you make it. But you believe this Vincent guy? Beyond a doubt?"

"I wouldn't say beyond a doubt," I admitted. "But I have a feeling he's telling the truth."

"And what's the deal with Daisy? She seems so nervous. I have trouble picturing her killing someone. But I guess you never really know."

"The Daisy I saw leading the cooking class wasn't the same Daisy we saw being pushed around by her mother at the competition. *That* Daisy could have poisoned someone. She took a huge risk by breaking into a crime scene and stealing evidence after all. I know I did the same thing, but why did *she* do it?"

"Juliet is right. You have to confess everything to Surly Steve and let him sort it all out."

"I know," I sighed.

"Did you tell him about your conversation with Eliot Thornfield?"

"I did!" I nodded excitedly. At least I got that part right.

"What did he say about it?"

"Not much. He was mostly annoyed that I was still butting into the investigation. But if he thought he was frustrated with me before, he'll hit the fan when he discovers just how much I interfered. Especially when he learns I knew about it last night when he was at the bar and didn't tell him. Oh, what have I done?" I moaned, sinking my head into my hands.

"You always do the right thing in the end. Even if you really mess up on the way there. And boy, do you mess up sometimes. You know, now that I think about it, if what Vincent says is true, LeClair sure went out of his way to reinvent himself. Like in a huge way."

"I guess he wanted to escape a childhood spent in foster care." I shrugged. "I understand that part."

"Yeah, but according to Vincent, he just took off for a

foreign country as a teenager. Without warning *and* ille-gally? Then he spent how many decades pretending he wasn't who he said he was? I feel like there's something more to it than he was just looking for a way out of foster care. And then you said Vicent went to Canada? Seems odd."

"Maybe they liked the idea of adventure?" I offered.

The more Wendy pointed it out, however, the more I realized I hadn't stopped to consider why teenagers would suddenly do something like that. "It sounded like LeClair had always been a con artist. Frequently talking his way out of sticky situations. According to Vincent, he always said he wanted to make something of himself."

"Sounds like we, I mean, Sheriff Mack, better track this guy down."

"Yeah! Get the truth!" Mystery replied, having suddenly reappeared to swipe her paw through the air like she'd give Vincent a good scratch to make him talk.

"I assume the Sheriff's Department could check into LeClair's background? His real background, of course? You're the private investigator." Wendy pointed at me. "Shouldn't you know how to do this?"

"Given that Sebastian was in foster care as a child and left before he turned 18, I don't know that the information would be that easy to locate. And this was long before social media, obviously, so that's out. Sheriff Mack didn't seem to think it was that important anyway, so I might have to convince him to check into it."

"I'm pretty sure he'll see this differently when you tell him the truth," Wendy reminded me.

"Oh, yeah, good point," I responded, my shoulders slumping in defeat. "If I go to jail, someone will have to look after Clara and Mystery, keep them updated. Maybe drive them around in the bus."

"Let's not get ahead of ourselves now," Wendy said gently. "You're 100% in big trouble for taking those things from LeClair's room, but we don't know for certain that it's evidence or what it even means. Isn't there anyone else who could identify him? Aside from you?" Wendy asked.

I shook my head. "The bar was quiet last night. I doubt the other patrons were paying attention. Oh!" I snapped my fingers. "Sam, the bartender who was there before me. He's the one who pointed Vincent out. He would know what he looked like. And maybe Vincent told him something, too!"

"There you go. Now we're getting somewhere."

When Juliet and Clara returned, Wendy and I looked up, hopefully.

"Just so you know, I'm still mad at you," Juliet said.

"I understand," I whispered, gazing at the floor.

"But you can *start* to make it up to me by going to the Sheriff's Department first thing in the morning and confessing it all to Sheriff Mack. Not because I want you punished, but because it's the right thing to do."

I nodded. "I agree."

"And I don't care if that means you get arrested."

"I understand," I whispered.

"Ask them about Thanksgiving!" Clara exclaimed.

"Clara, this is hardly the time!" I responded crossly.

"What is hardly the time?" Juliet asked.

"It's not important, really," I maintained. When Juliet glared at me, I sighed in resignation. "I told Clara we could have Thanksgiving at our house this year and invite both of you. And now she's insisting I tell you about it. Sorry. I know the timing is horrible."

"We'll see how things go tomorrow," Juliet said in a way

that gave me hope she really could forgive me. "Do you want me to make dessert?"

"I wouldn't want to assume," I added. "I'm sure everyone asks you to do that."

"We'll see," was all she said.

At that point, Mystery walked over to Juliet and stared up at her. "Maybe not pumpkin pie, though, huh?"

I did *not* repeat that out loud.

TWENTY

I CAN EXPLAIN EVERYTHING!

I slept horribly, tossing and turning all night over what I'd done. But when I finally decided to get up, it was so early that when I called the sheriff's department, they told me they didn't expect Sheriff Mack for another hour. That gave me one more hour of freedom to sew up some loose ends before I put my future in the hands of law enforcement.

I could go to the hotel to check Sam's work schedule and ask Sheriff Mack to follow up with him about Vincent. Then, maybe. Just, maybe. But only maybe, a staff member or spirit could give me one last clue. After that, who knew where I would be?

Considering I was the only one who could communicate with the spirits, I felt I owed it to Juliet to give it a final shot. I desperately needed her to forgive me, and I desperately needed to uncover the real killer.

Driving over the Grand Avenue Bridge toward the hotel, I barely noticed what was typically one of my favorite sights: the waking sun greeting the town while a a curtain of steam rises from the Hot Springs. I recalled one of my first days in Glenwood Springs when I went for an early morning run and paused at the top of the bridge in awe of the incredible scene before me. There was nowhere else in the world that looked like this, and it was inspiring every time I saw it. I only hoped I wasn't in jail for so long that I forgot what it looked like.

As usual, I parked in the employee parking lot and entered through the back door. I cut through the kitchen, and as I greeted two ghosts and the living staff, I paused for a moment and thought about how four suspects were spotted in the kitchen near the locked refrigerator before the contest. Why was it always that way? Why couldn't it be just one suspect who got caught in the beginning and confessed immediately?

I stared at the refrigerator and examined the lock. Of course, the sheriff's deputies had already gone over this inch by inch. Sheriff Mack indicated there were too many finger-prints on it to single anyone out. The lock was still in working order, and there was no sign it was tampered with. The kitchen staff were the only ones who had access to the key. Could one of *them* have opened it? What if they opened it but forgot to lock it again? The killer could have witnessed that and made their move.

When I approached the administrative offices, I found Gerald hard at work already. What would he think when he learned I had taken the master key and broke into a room? I would lose my bartending job.

And even if I didn't go to jail for a long time, why would anyone hire me as a private investigator ever again? I'd be a felon. How did I manage to screw up something so great in such a big way?

"Good morning, Gerald. Do you know when Sam is coming in today?"

"Uhhh, I think he's on vacation," he mumbled, not looking up from the file he was reading.

"Vacation? No! That can't be!" I cried. "Are you sure?"

He pushed his glasses up to get a better look at the staff schedule. "Yep. He's on vacation for the next week. I think he said he was going to the Bahamas."

That was not what I wanted to hear. I wandered into the lobby, pondering my next move, and checked my watch. Thirty minutes until Sheriff Mack was due in the office. Thirty minutes left of my freedom. Could I reach Sam in the Bahamas? Although I wasn't sure what good it would do.

"Psst! Psst! Breather! Boy, am I glad to see you!"

"What is it, Charles?" I asked crossly. I kind of, sort of blamed him for talking me into breaking into LeClair's room in the first place. I get that it was my responsibility to say no, but he still wasn't my favorite ghost at the moment.

"You have to go into LeClair's room again. It's an emergency."

"Nope. Nope. Nope." I shook my head. "I am not doing that again."

"I swear to you, you have to see something."

"I don't have to see *anything*. Do you realize I'm probably headed to jail this morning because I already broke in there and took evidence? I'll be going to the Sheriff's Office shortly. Just tell me what this supposed emergency is, and I'll let him know when I get there."

"It will be too late by that time. Please, you've got to come quick."

I glanced back at Gerald's office, but he was on the phone. What if this really was an emergency, and I ignored Charles, and something horrible happened? "Why don't you just tell me what it is? Then I can decide if it's an emergency," I offered.

"Oh, forget it," he said grumpily right before disappearing.

Nope! I wasn't falling for it. That was the old me. The new me didn't get involved with these shenanigans. No more unnecessary risks. Especially when it concerned my friends. I stomped toward the kitchen, prepared to drive straight to the Sheriff's Department. But that dastardly little devil that often sits on my shoulder whispered in my ear about what might happen if there was truly an emergency and I failed to do something about it.

I was the only one who could talk to ghosts, after all. What if it was an actual emergency, and I ignored it? Then, not only would I be responsible for losing potential evidence that could clear Juliet, but I'd be responsible for failing to help out when only I could.

"I can't believe I'm doing this," I muttered as I returned to get the master key. Maybe I could have Gerald open the door. I could tell him my suspicions, and he could handle it. Only now, he wasn't in his office. Of course. With a heavy sigh, I grabbed the master key, cursing all the way to LeClair's room.

This was definitely one of those times when I hated being a ghost whisperer. I decided to open the door just a little crack, stick my head in, make sure there was nothing wrong, and leave. In fact, I'd even admit the whole thing to Sheriff Mack just to cover my bases. He might commend me for smart thinking. Yeah, right, I laughed to myself.

As I opened the door, the butterflies in my stomach felt more like bats than pretty insects while my heart thumped wildly. The room was exactly as I'd left it yesterday. The bed was still neatly made, and the curtains were drawn. Just as I thought. No emergency. That was the last time I listened to Charles.

My eyes fell on the vent cover where I'd left it. What if I missed something in my haste yesterday? I could double-check the vent to see if there was anything else. If there were, I wouldn't touch it! But I could replace the cover, and then I was off to see Sheriff Mack. I drew in a sharp breath, trying to steady my nerves as I crossed the room, my eyes sweeping the area, looking for anything out of place.

But how I kept from screaming when I saw the hand poking out from behind the far side of the bed, I would never know. I crept forward, praying it wasn't what I thought it was. It had to be a prank, right? Some kind of Halloween prop that had been here the entire time but I missed it when I was here yesterday. My worst fears were confirmed when I rounded the corner of the bed.

Vincent lay on the floor, his eyes wide and glassy, staring blankly at the ceiling while the front of his shirt was soaked with blood. A pie server protruded from his chest, the handle glinting in the dim light from the bedside lamp. I stumbled backward, my hand over my mouth, stifling a scream.

The room spun as the reality of what I was seeing sank in. Vincent, who just yesterday was introducing himself as an old friend of Sebastian's, was now dead at my feet. I bent down to double-check that it was indeed a pie server in his chest when the door flew open.

"Put your hands up!" Sheriff Mack shouted.

The sudden shock of seeing him sent me spinning while my foot caught on the edge of the bed. I stumbled and waved my arms uselessly as I fought to keep my balance, only to then trip over the throw rug, where I landed hard on my backside with an undignified yelp. Sheriff Mack stared at me, his expression a mix of shock and exasperation as he took in the scene - me sprawled on the floor next to Vincent's lifeless body.

"What in Sam Hill?" he uttered.

"I can explain everything!" I exclaimed.

TWENTY-ONE

CAUGHT IN THE ACT

"What... What... What are you doing here?" he spluttered, his voice a mix of shock and suspicion. Yikes. I'd never seen him at a loss for words.

"I... I just found him like this. I swear," I explained, my voice cracking.

"Who is that?" he demanded, reaching out his hand to help me up.

"It's the guy I was telling you about yesterday." I jabbed my finger at him. "Sebastian LeClair's childhood friend, Vincent."

Sheriff Mack squinted at me. "Why are you here in the first place? And did you touch anything?"

"You know I didn't kill him, right?" I begged.

"From what I can tell, he's been dead for at least several hours. Unless, of course, you killed him earlier and came back to check on the body."

"Of course I didn't!" I exclaimed while Sheriff Mack rolled his eyes in my direction. He knew I didn't do it. Yet my brain raced, searching for a plausible explanation to give him as to why I was in Sebastian LeClair's room kneeling over a body in the first place.

He scowled in frustration. "You realize that I can just see the gears turning in your brain," he commented, circling a finger next to his own head, "trying to come up with an explanation as to what you're doing in a crime scene with yet another body?"

I gulped. There was no way out of this one but finally admitting the truth. "I was looking for clues."

"Clues?" his voice rose. "This is an active crime scene! You can't just break in here whenever you feel like playing detective, looking for random clues!"

"Now, hear me out," I said, cringing when my voice trembled. If I thought I was in trouble before, this was a whole other level of trouble. "One of the hotel spirits insisted I check out the room. He said there was an emergency."

Sheriff Mack cut me off with a sharp gesture. "A spirit, huh? Well, your spirit just landed you in a whole heap of trouble. I got a call from the hotel staff saying that they thought they saw someone sneaking into this room, and my first thought was it could be you. But then I told myself, no, I made it clear to her she wasn't to interfere in this investigation, especially since her best friend is a suspect. Yet here you are, kneeling over the body. And I *should* arrest you! Why must you constantly put me in this position?"

He was as mad as I had ever seen him. And I definitely saw him mad before, usually at me. Sure, he drove me crazy, but I still considered him a friend, and now, like Juliet, I'd put him in a difficult position.

"What I know," he said, his tone softening slightly, "is that you have a habit of sticking your nose where it doesn't belong. And this time, it might have gotten you into more trouble than you can handle." He rubbed his forehead like I was giving him a headache. "You'll have to give an official statement."

I gulped when I remembered that I was supposed to confess this morning anyway. "I have to talk to you. About something else, I mean."

"What now?" he snapped, still grumpy.

"It's about the case. It's not about this, of course," I admitted, waving my hand in Vincent's direction. "It's about something else."

"Holly, I don't have time for anything else right now."

"But this is important," I insisted.

"Wait outside in the hallway with the deputy. And don't leave! I'll talk to you when I can," he said, steering me to the door. When I stepped outside, I gave a small smile to the deputy, who returned it with a stiff gaze of suspicion.

"I didn't do it," I added. "In case you were wondering."

He continued staring wordlessly at me. Okey dokey, no small talk then.

I waited silently while the investigative team and the coroner filed into the room. While I may not have been talking, my mind still reeled with possibilities. What if Daisy did this? What if she came back for more evidence, found Vincent in the room, and killed him to keep him quiet? Perhaps he surprised her, and she panicked and stabbed him!

As I waited, deputies and other law enforcement wandered in and out of the room. Every time the door opened, I tried to catch a glimpse inside to see what was happening, but too many people were blocking my line of sight.

Then it hit me. What if Vincent had the evidence he took from me in his pocket? It wouldn't get me off the hook, but at least it could help Juliet. Even though I still didn't know if it truly was evidence. It would be better than nothing.

"Excuse me," I turned to the deputy, who continued glaring at me. He was very good at that. "This will sound like a weird request, but could you ask them to check the victim's pockets and--"

"Ms. Daniel!" the sheriff rebuked me so sharply I jumped. "What are you doing?"

"I was just asking--"

"Follow me!" he ordered while stomping down the hall, his long legs forcing me to scramble to keep up. When we reached the end of the hallway, he pulled me out of the way into the small area next to the ice machine.

"I'm asking you again: what were you doing in that room this morning? And don't tell me you were looking for clues. I want specifics."

"I should start at the beginning then. And you won't like it, but I swear I only had the best intentions."

"No doubt," he said sarcastically.

"Charles, a hotel ghost, told me he saw Sebastian hiding something in his room."

"You said he told you there was an emergency."

"That was only this morning," I corrected him.

"What do you mean that was this morning? That doesn't make sense. Oh, don't tell me..."

I nodded sheepishly. "Yesterday, Charles told me that he watched LeClair hide something before he died. And it was still in the room because you hadn't found it."

"Do you really want to confess to something I can arrest you for?" he warned me.

"No, not really. But I have to. I promised Juliet."

"Proceed."

"After Charles told me LeClair hid something, I argued that I should go to you right away and let you know."

"And yet you didn't."

"No, he talked me into going in there first," I mumbled.

"Because you wanted to see what it was before I did."

"Pretty much," I responded. How was it that everyone knew me so well?

"What did he hide?"

"It was a picture of three friends, boys to be exact, and a note that said "I Know Who You Are.""

"You realize that by removing evidence from a crime scene, you may have compromised the case and that when we catch the real killer, they can't use that against him or her? Is it at your house or in the VW?"

"Uhhh, neither."

"So you *did* leave it here?"

"No, but I can tell you why I accidentally took it."

"This ought to be good," he said, shaking his head.

"While I was searching the room for additional clues, Daisy broke in." That got his attention.

"What did Daisy say when she saw you?"

"She didn't say anything. I hid."

"You know, if this were anyone else telling me this, I'd never believe them."

"So you believe me?" I asked hopefully, but he didn't respond other than to glare at me for the 800th time. "Okay, well, Daisy stole something."

"What did she steal?"

"I'm not sure."

"Setting that aside for a moment. I'll question Daisy

later. That still doesn't explain why you stole evidence *acci-dentally*, as you claim."

"I got so rattled when Daisy came in the room that I shoved the picture and the note in my apron pocket. And right after she left, I darted out too, before I could get caught."

"So the evidence is still here in the hotel?" he asked.

"Only if it's on Vincent's body." He pinched the bridge of his nose again, let out a long, exasperated sigh, and fixed me with a look that made me feel about two inches tall. I waited for him to say something, to yell at me, but all I got was silence, which was worse than yelling. But I pressed on. "When I met Vincent at the bar, and he told me about Sebastian, I showed him the picture and the note. Which, by the way, matched the handwriting of the note left on my bus. He confirmed it was a picture of him and Sebastian when they were kids."

Sheriff Mack knocked his hand against the ice machine, making me jump. His face turned red as he struggled to remain composed. "Of all the reckless, irresponsible..." he trailed off, turning away to pace next to the ice machine. When he finally faced me again, his jaw was clenched so tight a muscle ticked in his cheek. "Do you have any idea what you've done? This isn't one of your ghost investigations - this is a murder case. That evidence could have been crucial to catching our killer, and now it's gone. Not only did you contaminate my crime scene, but you may have lost our best lead." He leaned forward, pointing at me. "You better hope we find that evidence on Vincent's body. This may be the worst mistake you've made since I've known you, and that's saying something."

In all the time I had known him, he never said anything quite that harsh. But if I ruined the murder investigation, I guess I deserved it. Thankfully, I was saved by the bell, at least for the moment anyway, when his phone rang.

"Mack here," he answered. "I'll be right there," he grunted. "I have an actual emergency I have to attend to. I'll deal with you later," he said, pushing past me and stomping away, leaving me to wonder if I would have any friends left in this town when this was all over.

TWENTY-TWO
THE RECEIPT

The sudden crash of ice cubes hitting the metal bin in the ice maker yanked me from my trance. What was I supposed to do now? Sheriff Mack said I had to give an official statement, but where? And when? Should I just stand around and wait to be arrested? He knew where I lived. I could go home and wait there. What an awkward situation. But before I could decide my next step, my phone buzzed with texts from Juliet and Wendy.

Wendy: Where are you?

Juliet: Are you with Sheriff Mack?

Juliet: I just heard they found a body at the Red Castle Hotel!

Me: Yeah, about that....

Wendy: Don't tell me...

Juliet: You promised you'd see Sheriff
Mack this morning and confess everything!

Me: Oh, I did that!

Juliet: So you're with him now?

Me: Uhhh, no, I'm at the hotel. But it's not
like I killed the guy or anything.

Wendy: The guy?

Me: Remember that guy I told you about?
Vincent.

Juliet: Get over to the bookstore. Now!

I wasn't going home after all! I was going to the bookstore. But before I could leave the building, another ghost summoned me just as I stepped from the entryway. It was a spirit I only saw occasionally and whose name I couldn't remember.

Given his clothing style, I assumed he died sometime in the 1990s. He wore baggy jeans with a plaid flannel shirt tied around his waist, and his Kurt Cobain-style hair hung across his face while a Walkman clipped to his belt played music only he could hear. I wondered what listening to the same cassette for several decades was like.

"Psst! Psst! C'mere!" he said, waving at me. I pointed to myself as if he'd be talking to any other living being.

"Hi," I told him. "I'm kind of in a hurry..."

"You've been asking around about that LeClair guy, right? You should know I saw that pretty guy from TV arguing with him in the courtyard. It got super messy, man, and they threw the pretty guy out."

"Pretty guy? The pastor?"

"Yeah, that's him."

"They were fighting, as in throwing punches?"

"Dude, it wasn't like a real fight or whatever. These guys were total amateurs - no one even threw a decent punch. But man, they were all up in each other's faces, pushing and yelling like crazy. Then LeClair totally shoved the pastor, and it was like something out of a movie - the guy went flying into this couple's lunch table. Food everywhere, plates crashing, total chaos. That's when security had to come break it up. It was pretty bogus."

"Did they say anything while they were fighting? What was the ruckus about?" I asked.

"It was totally intense," he explained, absently fiddling with his Walkman as he leaned against the wall, his flannel shirt swaying in a nonexistent breeze. "That pastor guy cornered LeClair in the middle of the courtyard, and man, he was seriously losing it - something about getting screwed over in some deal, but like, the acoustics in this place are wonky when you're dead, so I couldn't catch all of it." He brushed his long hair from his face with a translucent hand, adding, "But LeClair was being all whatever about it, like the pastor was overreacting - classic rich guy move, you know what I'm saying?"

"I think so?" I responded right before he shrugged and disappeared without a sound.

I paused momentarily, pondering why Sebastian and the pastor would have been arguing that seriously when I remembered, I was supposed to meet the girls.

I double-timed it to the bookstore, still mulling over what the ghost told me. If Pastor Greg and Sebastian were angry enough to engage in a physical fight, was Greg angry enough to kill him? And especially in public like that. I had to think that wouldn't look good for him as a pastor. What if his parishioners knew he was behaving like that? I must learn more about this fight.

The moment I set foot in the bookstore, Wendy and Juliet pounced.

"Where have you been?" Juliet scolded. "You were fixin' to give me the vapors!"

"Sorry about that," I explained. "A ghost in the hotel, whose name I can never remember, stopped me on my way out the door, and get this, he saw Sebastian LeClair and Pastor Greg arguing. They came to blows in the hotel court-yard, and security had to escort the pastor from the premis-es!" I paused expectantly, certain they'd be shocked.

"Holly!" Wendy chided.

"What?"

"The body?" Juliet bellowed, throwing up her hands.

"Oh. Yeah. Sorry about that. I have a lot going on right now, you know."

"Why were you at the hotel when you were supposed to be confessing to Sheriff Mack?" she accused.

"For the record," I added before she could get any madder, "I told him everything. After I discovered the body, of course." If I thought Sheriff Mack was shocked at finding me with Vincent's body, that was nothing compared to the way Wendy and Juliet were staring at me. "You said it was on the news. Did they give any details?"

"They only said the coroner was on the scene, and insiders were telling them it was another body."

"How did he die? And why did *you* find him?" Juliet asked. She was worried, which I took as a good sign that she wouldn't be mad at me forever.

"You won't like this. Sheriff Mack sure didn't. But I

stumbled across the body in Sebastian's room. He was stabbed with a pie server."

"I don't really know what to say at this point," Wendy replied. "Part of me is stunned. But part of me so totally knows you that I almost expect something this convoluted."

"But what did Sheriff Mack say when you confessed to breaking into LeClair's room and stealing evidence?" Juliet asked. My poor friends. Always having to help sort out my messed up life.

I sighed heavily. It hurt my heart to recall how angry and upset he was. "Furious isn't even close," I told them. "But before he could decide what to do with me, he got an emergency call and had to leave. And that's when you texted me. I'm honestly not sure what happens next. I guess I wait for him to arrest me."

"Oh, Holly," Juliet sighed, pity crossing her features. "Why must you repeatedly put yourself in these situations? You live your life like it was some kind of made for TV drama."

"Holy smokes, don't hate me for changing the subject, but I just remembered something," Wendy cut in. "I overheard customers the other day talking about how *they* heard Pastor Greg was getting a TV show."

"Isn't his service already live-streamed?" I asked.

"Yes, and I missed most of the conversation, but what I caught sounded like it was something different. It was beyond just streaming the service for television. I didn't think much of it at the time but now that you've brought up the fight..."Wendy paused to think. "What if Sebastian and Greg's fight had something to do with it? LeClair had a TV show after all..." she trailed off as we stared at her in confusion. "I don't know, it's just something that jumped into my head."

"I can check into it." I nodded. "And I should do it before Sheriff Mack comes for me."

"Please be careful!" Juliet warned.

"Aren't I always?" I asked.

"No!" they exclaimed in unison.

When I left the bookstore, I intended to walk back to the hotel and find Sheriff Mack. But I reasoned if I was about to be arrested, I should get coffee first. And perhaps a scone. A cinnamon scone!

I reversed course and headed to the coffee shop two doors away. But just as I reached for the doorknob, Daisy Thompson herself walked out. We stood frozen, staring at each other in shock.

"You better not be here to harass me again!" she exclaimed.

"I wasn't harassing you the other day. I was just curious about a few things," I insisted. "By the way, have you talked to the police yet?"

"The police? Why would I talk to the police?"

I hesitated to tell her. Vincent's body wouldn't be the only one they found today if Sheriff Mack discovered I talked to Daisy before he did. But here she was, right in front of me. How could I pass up the opportunity? But Daisy had other plans and started to walk away.

"I saw you!" I exclaimed before my chance to solve the murder disappeared with her.

"I don't know what you're talking about," she insisted, as she continued walking.

"I saw you in Sebastian LeClair's room."

"Excuse me?" she snarled, spinning on her heel and approaching me so fast I took a step back. "You saw nothing."

"I saw you because I was there too."

"No, you weren't," she laughed.

"I was hiding in the bathroom. I watched you take a slip of paper from the desk drawer."

Daisy paled and immediately reverted to her habit of fingernail chewing. "And you called the cops on me?"

"No, not at the time. But I mentioned it to Sheriff Mack when I saw him this morning."

"Why were you talking to him this morning?"

"Because I went back to LeClair's room and found the body."

"Body?" she hollered in shock. "What body?" Now, she was the one who stepped back. That wasn't the reaction I was expecting. She was genuinely surprised. "Have you been drinking?" she asked, smelling the air between us.

"I found Vincent's body."

"Vincent? Who's Vincent?" she asked. "You're scaring me. I don't know what's wrong with you, but I'm leaving."

"No, wait, please! Just hear me out this time. The police will contact you at any moment, and I may be your best hope."

"But I didn't do anything wrong."

"You broke into a crime scene and removed evidence," I reminded her.

"Apparently, you broke in too!"

"I know. And believe me, I'm already in trouble. But maybe I could help you here." No, I couldn't really help her, but I needed answers!

Her shoulders slumped as she gave in. "I broke into his room to steal the receipt I got from the Village Inn."

"Village Inn? I don't get it."

"I bought a pie from the Village Inn for the competition, and LeClair caught me!"

My mouth formed into a shocked O. "You bought a pie to enter in the contest? I don't understand."

"I'm a horrible baker!" she cried, chewing on her fingernails even harder. How did she have any left?

"But you teach cooking at the adult learning center. Your mom owns a restaurant."

"I know that! But I'm better at teaching than I am cooking."

"Then why enter the contest in the first place?"

"Because my mother made me! And if I came in last place like I knew I would, she would be livid. I was desperate, and those pies are delicious."

She was right. Their pies were good.

"But how did LeClair get your receipt?"

"He was at the counter drinking coffee when I went in to pick up the pie I ordered. I didn't even notice him at first, but he sure noticed me. He waited until I got outside and grabbed the receipt from my hands. He told me if I entered that pie, he'd turn me in. So I promised him I wouldn't. But he insisted on keeping the receipt as evidence."

"But you entered it anyway? And that's why Juliet saw you arguing before the competition!" I exclaimed, while Daisy nodded tearfully.

"You told me you were in the kitchen hiding from your mother. Was that a lie?"

"No!" she wailed. "I really was trying to get away from her. But look! I still have the receipt!" Sure enough, she pulled a receipt from her pocket, and it looked like the piece of paper she had taken from the desk drawer in LeClair's room. I examined it closely, and she was right. She purchased a chocolate cream pie two days before the competition.

I didn't want to believe her. I wanted to think that she

killed LeClair and Vincent and that as soon as the authorities figured it out, Juliet would be off the hook.

"You have to believe me!" she begged.

"I do," I sighed in resignation.

And as if my morning wasn't already dramatic and troublesome enough, my stomach dropped when Sheriff Mack pulled up to the curb in front of us.

Why did he have such impeccable timing? His expression darkened when he stepped out of the SUV, and I could practically see his blood pressure spiking.

"Really?" he exclaimed, his voice carrying that dangerous edge I'd come to recognize all too well.

Before I could stammer out an explanation, Daisy's eyes went wide with panic. She looked from Sheriff Mack to me, then back to Sheriff Mack, and something in her expression shifted.

Without warning, she spun around and sprinted up 6th Street, her shoes thumping frantically against the pavement as she disappeared around the corner. Sheriff Mack shot me a look that could have melted steel before taking off after her.

"She's innocent!" I shouted after him, but of course, they kept going. Hey, if Daisy was running, I could too. Only I didn't actually run. I walked back to the hotel, got in my bus and headed for Pastor Greg's church.

Daisy's disappearing stunt had bought me a little extra time, and I had to take full advantage of it before *I* was the one Sheriff Mack had to chase.

TWENTY-THREE

A QUARTER MILLION MOTIVES

I was in more trouble than I'd ever been in with Sheriff Mack, but I was also running out of time. I couldn't bear to lose Juliet's friendship, and there was a killer at large in our community. I had to do everything I could before Sheriff Mack locked me up and threw away the key.

So many clues pointed at Pastor Greg, that I had to talk to him again. He was in the kitchen when he wasn't supposed to be, he was thrown out of the hotel for fighting with LeClair, and what was up with this new TV show the customers in Wendy's shop were talking about? I needed more answers, and I needed them fast.

"Hi there, could you tell me where I would find Pastor Greg?" I asked a man who I assumed given his uniform and tool belt was the church janitor or a handyman. Or both.

"He isn't here."

"Oh. Okay. That's too bad. Do you know when he'll be back?"

"Nope. Is it important? There's a list of emergency numbers on the wall," he said, pointing to a flyer on the bulletin board.

This man wasn't a talker! "I wouldn't call it an emergency. If I leave my card with you, could you see that he gets it?"

"Sure." He studied the card I gave him. "Are you here about LeClair's murder?"

"In a manner of speaking." Did this guy know something none of the rest of us knew?

"Is the Pastor a suspect?" he pressed.

"Why do you ask that?"

"Because the last time I saw him with Sebastian LeClair, their argument got so heated, I almost called the cops."

"What were they arguing about?"

"What does anyone argue about? Money."

I almost expected him to add 'duh' at the end of that. "Money?" I asked.

"Yeah. Didn't you know? What kind of investigator are you?"

"Of course, I knew it was about *money*," I claimed. "But could you tell me exactly what happened between them? When you witnessed the argument, I mean."

"Sebastian LeClair promised Pastor Greg they could work together on a new TV show."

So Wendy's assumption it was about a *different* TV show was correct! "Pastor Greg's services were already televised. What more did he want?"

"LeClair told him that he knew people in the *industry*," the janitor said with air quotes. "Pitched him an idea for a reality television show. You know, like his chef show only with the pastor. LeClair said if Greg invested the money, he had the connections."

"Let me guess," I said, leaning forward conspiratorially. "It never happened," I whispered.

He nodded. "You guessed right. Pastor Greg was furious, and they fought over it numerous times."

"How much money are we talking here?"

"Hold on to your hat." He paused dramatically. "250,000."

"Dollars?" I exclaimed so loudly it echoed in the chapel lobby.

"Well, of course, dollars. What did you think I meant? Pennies?"

"That seems like an absurd amount of money. Did Greg give it to him?"

"Why do you think they were always fighting?"

I was stunned. A quarter million dollars was a lot of motive. About $250,000 worth of motive.

"Bill! Bill!" a young man called out as he ran down the hallway.

"What is it now?" the janitor asked grumpily.

"One of the upstairs toilets is overflowing!"

"Sorry, but I gotta go! I'll tell Pastor Greg to contact you," he said, waving my card in front of me.

"Thank you," I told him.

I wandered back to my bus, mulling over everything we'd learned about Pastor Greg today. $250,000! That was insane. No wonder they were duking it out at the hotel. For that kind of money, I might too.

"Hey Gerald, what's up?" I asked when my phone rang with a call from my manager.

"Sebastian LeClair's publicist has booked the bar for an impromptu Celebration of Life service this afternoon. I know this is super last minute, but is there any--"

"Yes!" I exclaimed.

"I didn't even finish," he protested.

"You were going to ask me to help out at the bar."

"Oh. Uh. Yeah."

"My answer is still yes," I insisted.

"Great, I'll see you at 2:00."

Assuming I wasn't in jail by then, I thought as I hung up. I kept expecting Sheriff Mack to jump out of the shadows and arrest me, but I hadn't heard anything new, so planned to continue investigating, for now anyway.

Given the mystery still surrounding Sebastian LeClair's death, I was certain there would be a ton of people at the service. Everyone will show up just to be able to say they were there. And, the best part was I could talk to people about the case without looking like I was really talking to people about the case. If you catch my drift. Oh, this is fabulous. Why didn't I think of it before?

TWENTY-FOUR
LECLAIR'S LAST COCKTAIL

Just as I had predicted, the service was packed with people. The hotel transformed the normally elegant bar space into what could only be described as a shrine to Sebastian LeClair's ego. Enormous posters from his TV show covered the walls while a slideshow of his "greatest culinary moments" played on a loop on a big-screen TV.

Many of the attendees who I suspected were hoping for drama more than anything else, were all clutching a complimentary "LeClair's Last Cocktail" a dubiously named specialty drink that the bar had created for the occasion.

A table near the fireplace groaned under the weight of dishes supposedly inspired by LeClair's recipes, though I doubted the man would have approved of the grocery store cheese plate or the questionable-looking mini quiches.

The crowd was a mixture of those who appeared to be treating this like a networking event, complete with business card exchanges and others who were dramatically sharing their "personal connections" to the chef - most of which seemed to involve having eaten at his restaurant once when they visited New York City or watching his show reli-giously.

Naturally, numerous reporters were on hand, hoping for a big scoop. Given what happened at the pie baking competition, I'm sure they assumed anything could happen. And they would be right! The whole scene felt less like a memorial and more like a poorly planned fan convention.

"Holly! Finally!" Virginia, the librarian, exclaimed when she found me restocking cocktail napkins.

"Oh, hi! I was just in the library looking for you the other day," I told her.

"Yes, I got your message, and I apologize for not getting back to you right away. I hope it wasn't an urgent matter?"

"I wanted to talk to you about Eliot Thornfield."

"The author? What about him?"

"I was curious if you knew anything interesting about him. I know he's relatively new to town, and I'm also aware of the rumors that he claims to be a best selling author, yet no one has confirmed it?"

Virginia paused thoughtfully. "He is an odd one. But I have no complaints about him personally, just so you know," she exclaimed, lifting her hand like she was swearing an oath. "He spends a lot of time in the library, as you can imagine, and he's a model patron. He's polite, always puts the reference materials back where he found them, and when he uses the meeting room to interview people about Glenwood's history, he cleans it afterward. You don't want to know some of the things I've found in that room," Virginia explained with a shudder.

"Ewww. You're right. I don't want to know," I laughed. "What kind of books does he check out? Am I allowed to ask that, or is there some sort of librarian and reader confiden-tiality agreement?"

"Not that I'm aware of," she giggled. "It's all just history books. History of Glenwood, history of Colorado, Gold Rush history. Those types of things. The only one that wasn't related to history was a book on homeopathy. Something about natural treatment of burns."

"He was a contestant in the pie baking competition. I bet he burned himself making the tarte."

Virginia nodded. "Probably. Sorry, I couldn't be of more help."

"Not at all. I appreciate the information."

"I better get one of those specialty cocktails before they run out! See you around," she said with a wave.

I'm disappointed she didn't have more tea on Thornfield, but what was I expecting? That she'd confess he'd asked her for a step by step guide on how poisons worked?

"Good afternoon, Ms. Daniel," Sheriff Mack said, dropping a pair of handcuffs on the bar.

Uh oh.

"I don't suppose this could wait, could it?" I asked. "There are so many people here; Gerald desperately needs my help. I swear, I'll drive myself to the station the minute the service is over."

"Relax," he said, rolling his eyes at me. "I was only trying to make you sweat. I'm not arresting you... yet," he added when he saw me breathe a sigh of relief. "You seem to be talking to a lot of people this afternoon."

"There's a lot of people here."

"Anything useful you want to tell me?"

"What happened to Daisy?" I asked.

"That's a question, not a statement."

"I know, but..." I trailed off.

"We confirmed through the receipt and the restaurant that Daisy ordered the pie. The hostess also remembered overhearing an argument between Daisy and LeClair about how it violated the rules of the contest to purchase a pie."

"So Daisy is off the hook?" I asked.

"For now," he replied. "By the way, before you go blabbing to someone you shouldn't, we haven't made any of the details about Vincent, or his death, public. As far as anyone else is concerned, they think that some random stranger died at the hotel from natural causes."

"I noticed there still hasn't been much coverage of that," I pointed out.

"With good reason."

"Mum's the word," I said, pretending to zip up my lips. "Hey, what's going on there?" I asked, pointing across the room at a reporter attaching a microphone to Mabel's jacket.

"This should be interesting," Sheriff Mack mumbled as he moved closer to the action.

I was relieved it at least put his focus on someone else.

As the reporter signaled to the cameraman to start recording, Mabel fussed with her hair, making sure every one of them was still tucked tightly into the usual bun on her head.

"Ms. Winchester," the reporter began, "thank you for agreeing to this interview. You're the owner of the Mabel's Magical Preserves, right?"

"Yes, I am. Proud owner, I'd like to add!" she exclaimed, drawing herself up tall and straight.

"And you insist that you only use all natural, locally sourced ingredients in your products?"

"Absolutely!" Mabel declared, smiling broadly.

"And some of your products are enchanted..."

"Why, of course, but they all come with disclaimers, just so you know."

When the reporter shifted his stance and licked his lips,

I understood at that moment something was coming that Mabel hadn't anticipated when she agreed to the interview.

"Would you care to comment on the allegations made by the late Sebastian LeClair that the truth is, you often use artificial ingredients and your enchantments are, in his words, 'poppycock.'"

"I don't know where you heard that," Mabel stammered.

"But you were seen in public arguing with him about it."

"I don't know who's feeding you these stories, but I never argued with LeClair."

"But you were caught on camera. We have it right here," the reporter said while they cut in with the video of Mabel from social media, including, of course, Mabel's threats against LeClair.

By now, a crowd had gathered around them, and there was an audible gasp when they played the video. If I were Mabel, I'd insist the interview was over at that point. And yet, what could she do? The camera was rolling, and everyone was mesmerized by what was happening.

She looked about the room like a deer in the headlights, but then her demeanor shifted while her eyes flashed dangerously. "Allegations? That man wouldn't know a natural ingredient if it jumped up and bit him on the patootie!" She huffed, her cheeks flushing. "Everything in my jams and jellies comes straight from nature, just like my grandma taught me."

When the reporter nodded knowingly, I got the distinct feeling that there was more. And I was all for it. So was the rest of the room, which was now eerily silent. Whatever the police and I couldn't get from her, the reporter went after it. "There are rumors circulating that you may have, shall we say, *influenced* the results of the past three contests. Any comment on that?"

"Influenced? Are you saying I cheated?" she exclaimed nervously.

"We have a witness who claims they saw you in the kitchen before the pie judging began when it was off limits to the contestants. Can you tell us, Ms. Winchester, were you in the kitchen altering the pies so you could win? Did you accidentally poison it using witchcraft?"

Mabel's face underwent a series of expressions – shock, indignation, and then, surprisingly, resignation.

"I didn't kill anyone, and I don't use artificial ingredients in my products!"

The reporter leaned forward eagerly, his eyes wide. "So, you're admitting to *cheating* in the competition?"

Mabel looked as if she was ready to finally leave at that point but she saw Sheriff Mack move in close. She stood tall, a defiant glint in her eye. "Now, you listen here. I may have, well, *nudged* things in my favor a bit. A little spell here and there to make sure the judges appreciated the subtle flavors of my pies. But I did not, I repeat, did not use any artificial ingredients!"

"You placed a spell on the pies? Is that why you were in the kitchen?" the reporter asked, looking like he couldn't believe he got that lucky.

"No, you foolish boy! I was in the kitchen looking for Mr. Blackwood, the judge. I had already, uh, worked my magic on Tate and Holbrook, but Blackwood was nowhere to be found! And I assure you, I didn't poison or kill anyone! Now, get this microphone off me! The interview is over!" Mabel struggled with the microphone as a technician tried to help her untangle herself, but she swatted him away. Once she finally got free of it, she attempted to storm off in a huff only to be cut off by Sheriff Mack who signaled that they needed to talk.

See? I knew there would be drama.

While I was helping a waiter pick up a tray of dropped appetizers, Eliot Thornfield approached me. His eyes were bloodshot, and I assumed he had one too many LeClair's Last Cocktails to drink.

"So, Holly Daniel, Paranormal Private Investigator, we meet again," he said.

"Well, hello there. Nice to see you again."

"A little birdie told me you're a ghost whisperer."

"I am."

"You know what I'm thinking?" he asked.

"What's that?"

"It would be great to interview you about some history the local spirits may have shared with you? If you have time of course."

"Sure, that would be fun." I nodded.

"Great. I'll have my assistant call you to set up a time."

"Okay."

"Good afternoon, Mr. Mayor," Eliot said as the mayor walked by, but instead of returning the greeting, the mayor simply glared at us and made a harrumphing noise.

"That was strange," I pointed out. "Is it just me, or did he snub you?" I didn't want to appear gossipy, but that was weird.

Eliot cringed. "I think he's kind of mad at me."

"Why?"

"I was the one who pushed for adding LeClair as a judge."

"It was you? I wondered how that happened. But why?" I exclaimed. Why would he want LeClair as a judge? Unless, as I theorized earlier, he could have known LeClair from before? If Mystery and Wendy's suspicions were true, he could have murdered Sebastian over a secret recipe. "I have something to ask you," I pressed, "did you know Sebastian LeClair before you came to Colorado?"

"I know what you're thinking," he laughed. "And no, I didn't do it so I could poison him. At the time, I thought it would be good publicity for Glenwood, and the mayor did, too. A famous chef with a somewhat questionable temper moves to a quaint mountain town to settle down and then judges a local pie-baking competition. I thought it would be very appealing to the fans. How was I supposed to know he'd die on camera?"

"It would have been good publicity. If he hadn't died anyway. Hey, real quick while you're here, there was a witness who saw LeClair scolding you in the kitchen the night before the contest. What was that about?"

"Oh. Yeah," he chuckled uneasily. "He caught me turning in my pie at the last possible second and followed me into the kitchen to lecture me about punctuality and professionalism," Eliot explained, while his leg twitched with annoyance at the memory. "He claimed that being on time was just as important as the quality of the pie, and he threatened to have me disqualified if I was going to be so unprofessional about the whole thing. It was so ridiculous."

"He made friends wherever he went, didn't he?" I pointed out.

"He sure did. Now, I should go say hello and try to smooth things over with the mayor. I still have a lot of information I need to get from him for my book, and my publisher will kill me if I screw that up. But I'll call you about an interview!" he said.

"Please do!" I responded.

The remainder of the afternoon went as one might expect when you mix free food, strong drinks, and a room full of small town citizens trying to one-up each other with their Sebastian LeClair stories. Along with the rest of the staff, I called on ride shares for tipsy guests, cleaned up spilled drinks, and dodged the occasional flying appetizer when gestures became too animated.

A woman in designer heels broke not one but two wine glasses, all the time insisting she had no idea how it happened because she was perfectly sober. The "LeClair's Last Cocktail" turned out to be particularly potent, leading to increasingly loud declarations of "what Sebastian meant to me" from people who'd clearly never met him.

By the time the event wound down, the floors were sticky with spilled drinks, the food platters were decimated into sad crumbs, and many of the posters hung crookedly on the walls. If I were being honest, the whole thing was a fitting tribute to the man I'd met at the pool - overdone, self-important, and leaving a mess for others to clean up, including solving his murder.

As we closed up the bar and got ready to go home, I realized the only people I hadn't seen at the service were Daisy and Pastor Grey. I wanted to make sure Sheriff Mack knew that, too, but he disappeared after he led Mabel away to talk.

I knew she said she hadn't poisoned anyone on purpose, but what if her spell somehow went awry? The thought that she could have accidentally poisoned something made me shudder. Especially after I sampled her sour cherry preserves. Which were delicious, by the way!

All I wanted to do now was go home, sink into a steaming hot bubble bath, and keep my fingers crossed that everything could remain drama free for the remainder of the evening. Was that too much to ask?

TWENTY-FIVE
UNINVITED GUEST

I pulled into the garage, the familiar creak of the door closing behind me, a welcome sound after the day I just had. But Sheriff Mack hadn't locked me up and thrown away the key yet, so I was grateful for that.

As I climbed out of the bus, my mind still whirled with everything that happened. With the information I gathered, it would take a while to process it all. On my way into the house, still lost in thought, I nearly jumped out of my skin when a deep voice called out, "Good evening, Holly."

I spun around to see Pastor Greg standing at the edge of my driveway, his tall figure casting a long, ominous shadow in the fading twilight. My heart skipped a beat as I wondered how long he'd been waiting there. My first thought was to run. But could I outrun him? And where would I run to? I glanced at the door to the house, but it was locked. I couldn't get there, unlock it, then slam it shut before he caught up with me.

"Pastor Greg," I managed, trying to steady my voice. "I wasn't expecting you. What's up?" I flinched when it came out all squeaky. I should sound strong and unafraid, not like

I was worried he had murdered LeClair for ripping him off and maybe Vincent because he assumed he knew too much? Which meant I was next on the list.

When he took a step closer, I instinctively backed up. "I heard you were looking for me," he said. His usual charming demeanor was gone. Replaced by a cold and calculating tone and expression. "I thought I'd save you the trouble of tracking me down."

I swallowed hard, acutely aware of how quiet the neighborhood was at the moment. Didn't anyone need to go outside for their mail or to walk their dog? "I... I wanted to ask you about Sebastian LeClair," I explained.

He shifted his weight. "What about him?"

If I could keep him talking, someone had to come along before he killed me. "Someone told me you gave him $250,000 for a reality TV show."

Shock crossed his features. Then, his face clouded with anger. "Where did you hear that?"

"It doesn't matter," I said, desperate to sound more confident than I felt. "Is it true?"

Instead of confessing, he fixed me with an intense stare. "Was there anything else you wanted to ask me?"

"Why weren't you at the service today? Nearly everyone in town was there, which made your absence conspicuous."

"I had other matters to attend to," he said vaguely. "Not that it's any of your business. Now I have a question for you."

"Okay."

"How did you find that body in LeClair's room?"

I tried to keep my face neutral, but I'm sure it betrayed my terror. The only way he could have known about the body was if he killed Vincent.

As if reading my mind, he continued, "I have my

sources. Or were *you* the one who stabbed him with the pie server? I know you're quite chummy, if that's what you want to call it, with the sheriff," he said with a malevolent smile. "If he's covering for you, that could be terrible publicity for him in this town."

"Threatening a law enforcement officer is illegal, you know," I told him.

Pastor Greg only shrugged, then turned to leave. "Thank you for your time, Holly. I trust you'll keep our conversation in confidence. After all, we're both only trying to find the truth, aren't we?"

After he left, I sprinted for the house, threw myself inside, and locked the door behind me. I slumped against the door, breathing heavily. I had to call Sheriff Mack. At least he couldn't lecture me for seeking out trouble. This one came to me!

I pressed on his number and held my breath, hoping Pastor Greg was long gone. At least from my house.

"H. What's going on?" he answered on the first ring. "And don't think you're off the--"

"--Pastor Greg was just here and--"

"—what do you mean here?"

"Here at my house. He knows I found Vincent's body and that he was stabbed with a pie server."

"Is he still there?"

"No, he left, and that's when I called you."

"Are you inside?" he asked, sounding increasingly worried.

"Yes."

"Stay inside and keep the doors locked. I'll be right there."

"Okay," I said before sliding down the door and slumping on the floor.

I texted Wendy and Juliet because I couldn't think of anything else to do while I waited. They said they were on their way, too. Great. We could have a party.

"Holly, what's wrong?" Clara asked when she saw me sitting on the kitchen floor with my head in my hands.

"Did you notice anyone lurking in the yard earlier? A man?"

"No, I haven't seen a thing. Is someone here?"

"He was."

"Who was it?" she asked.

"Sebastian LeClair's killer."

Clara gasped. "Are you certain?"

"I'm mostly certain. I assume he came to threaten me. Maybe even to kill me? To make good on the note he left on my car? I really don't know why he didn't kill me when he had the chance."

"You better call Sheriff Mack!"

"I did. He's on his way."

Upon hearing that, Mystery, who had just walked into the kitchen, puffed out her tail, hissed, and ran up the stairs.

"Sheriff Mack is coming over?" Clara exclaimed, suddenly forgetting all about the killer who was just here. "I have to get ready. How does my hair look?" Then she took off too, presumably to comb her hair and put on some lipstick, I guess. How did my life get so weird?

Within minutes, Sheriff Mack appeared at the front door, followed closely by Wendy and Juliet.

"You had to invite the whole gang?" he asked.

I shrugged. "I was freaked out."

"What did he say exactly?" Sheriff Mack asked, his face a mixture of concern and professionalism.

I repeated my conversation with Pastor Greg the best I could remember it.

"He shouldn't know that. Any of that. It hasn't been reported anywhere."

"That's what scared me the most." I nodded.

"More than him showing up at your house?" Juliet exclaimed.

"Yeah? I think so? I don't know. It was just so freaky."

"Have you invited Sheriff Mack to Thanksgiving yet?" Clara asked, right before I gave her a salty look to tell her this was hardly the time.

The second time she asked, I snapped, "No!" which caused everyone but Clara to stare at me in confusion. Clara just pouted. "It's not the appropriate time. He has more important things to deal with at the moment," I explained, trying to soften the blow, which didn't work because she stomped away in a huff while I called after her, "Don't go away mad!"

"Seriously, what's happening here?" Sheriff Mack asked. "Why are you talking about me?"

"How do you know we're talking about you?" I asked.

"I'm the only *he* here."

"She does this all the time," Wendy responded. "Is this about the Thanksgiving thing?"

"Thanksgiving thing?" the sheriff asked.

"Seriously, guys? We have a killer to catch!" I reminded them.

But when they continued to stare at me wordlessly, I threw up my hands in defeat.

"Fine! I'm hosting Thanksgiving this year, and Clara wanted me to invite you," I nodded at the sheriff. "But I'm sure you have somewhere better to go anyway."

"Oh..." he hesitated, looking embarrassed. See, I knew it. Why would he want to come to my house for Thanksgiving, of all places? What a stupid question to ask. He was probably going to his girlfriend's house or something. I didn't even know if he had a girlfriend. I never asked.

"It's no big deal. Forget I asked. It was dumb," I stammered.

"No, it's not that," he said quickly. "It's just that I was taking my mom out to dinner. The annual Thanksgiving Buffet at the Red Castle Hotel."

"It's settled. You and your mom will join us!" Juliet proclaimed before I could tell him he'd probably prefer the buffet. "We would love to have you!"

"You would?" he asked.

"We would?" I responded.

"Yes!" Wendy said, pinching the back of my arm.

"That would be nice," he smiled. "My mom will love it."

"It's a date then!" Wendy exclaimed. If she didn't knock it off, she'd get more than a pinch from me.

"Now that it's settled, I have to find Pastor Greg. You stay home, and if you see anything that's the least bit suspicious, call me immediately, got it?"

"Got it," I told him.

"Keep an eye on her, you two," he told Wendy and Juliet before showing himself out the front door. "And lock the door behind me."

"Aye, aye, captain!" Wendy exclaimed, using a mock salute.

"What was that all about?" I asked.

"I don't know. It just seemed like the thing to do."

"At least he hasn't arrested you yet," Juliet pointed out.

"Don't think I forgot you stole evidence!" he said after sticking his head through the door again. "And I told you to lock this!"

"I'm locking, I'm locking!" Juliet responded while

shooing him out and immediately locking it this time. You'd think I would know better by now.

"Do you want us to stay with you?" Juliet asked.

"Nah, I'll be fine. Besides, I'm exhausted, and after this whole crazy day, I just want some quiet time."

"Call us if you need anything. Actually, call Sheriff Mack first, then call us."

"I will do that," I told them, showing them out the front door and locking it behind them. After making sure they got to their cars safely, I went through the house and double-checked every lock on every door and window. Clara and Mystery insisted they'd maintain the watch all night. I believed Clara, but I knew Mystery would be asleep before my head hit the pillow.

For good measure, right before I crawled into bed, I made sure Agnes, my trusty aluminum baseball bat, was beside me. If Pastor Greg or anyone else thought they were breaking in here, they had another thing coming.

TWENTY-SIX
THE THIRD FRIEND

The following morning, while eating breakfast and maintaining a watchful eye outside for any sign of Greg, my phone buzzed with a text notifying me that the book I reserved, *Thanksgiving for Beginners*, was available at the library. I might have two murders to solve and a creepy suspect stalking me, but I also had Thanksgiving dinner to prepare, and at times, I wondered which might be more difficult.

The dinner. Definitely the Thanksgiving dinner.

After assuring Clara I'd be extra careful - it was only the library, after all - I headed out. But, even I had to admit I was anxious. Pastor Greg showing up at my house hit a little too close to, well, home. Clara told me she saw a sheriff's car drive by twice last night, so I was relieved they were looking out for me.

I hadn't heard anything from Sheriff Mack this morning, which must mean Pastor Greg was still on the run. But how? Glenwood was a small town, how hard could it be to find a guy who liked to see himself on TV?

"HI, Virginia, I'm here to pick up the book I reserved," I told the librarian while peering through the bookshelves, fearing Pastor Greg might be lurking around every corner.

"Wonderful!" she exclaimed. "It's so frustrating when patrons reserve books but never show up. They just sit here, taking up space at the checkout desk," she said, waving her hand at the stack of books nearby.

"Does that happen a lot?" I asked. Why would someone reserve a book and not pick it up?

"Quite a bit. So, I've decided to impose a deadline from now on. You have two weeks, or it goes back to where it came from. Like this book, *Colorado: A History of The Gold Rush*. Eliot Thornfield told me he needed it expedited, so I went out of my way to track it down for him, yet there it sits. I've texted *and* called him to let him know it's in, but he still hasn't picked it up."

On a whim, I told her, "I'll take it to him."

"Really?" she asked.

"Sure, I was headed to his house anyway." Why did I say that? I lied to a librarian, of all people! That must be illegal or against the rules or something, right? But he told me he wanted to interview me for his book about Glenwood's haunted history. Wouldn't it be wild if I could arrange some actual ghost interviews for his book? Who else could do that for him but me? He may even have a ghost living in his house that I could talk to. It was perfect timing.

It also gave me a great excuse to follow up on my earlier questions that he never fully answered, like which books he authored. He would undoubtedly have copies of those on hand so I could put the mystery to rest once and for all.

THE TURNOFF for Eliot's house was a little tricky to find once the paved road turned into a dusty gravel road. I finally spotted it, though, after about a mile. His house was a small, aging structure with faded yellow clapboard siding that was peeling in places, revealing patches of bare wood underneath. A rickety porch stretched across the front while its roof sagged slightly, supported by columns that had seen better days. Two windows flanked the front door with faded curtains hanging behind the glass.

The overgrown yard was a tangle of wild grass and weeds, with the occasional flash of color from withering wildflowers. An ancient oak tree loomed over one corner of the house, its gnarled branches stretching over the roof.

My feet crunched along the gravel driveway as I approached the house, clutching his library book and taking in the rough scene before me. I hoped he wasn't too put out by my showing up unannounced, and to be honest, I was second guessing my decision to do it anyway.

The porch steps creaked as I approached the front door and raised my hand, knocking lightly on the door while a peeling paint fleck floated to the ground. When it creaked open a crack, I called out softly, "Hello?" When nothing happened, I pushed the door open a little more. "Hello?" I repeated, moving farther into the entryway.

I stepped inside to find a modest living room with fading floral wallpaper that clung stubbornly to the walls, its edges curled slightly in the corners. Dusty sunlight filtered through the old lace curtains, landing on a well-used couch and an armchair that had seen better days. A rickety coffee table sat in the center of the room, its surface marked with countless rings from coffee mugs. The air held the slightly musty scent common to older homes.

As my eyes scanned the living room, they landed on the far wall and my breath caught in my throat. Every inch was covered in a chaotic collage of newspaper clippings, magazine articles, and printed internet pages, all featuring Sebastian LeClair.

In addition to articles, both young and old, various photos of the celebrity chef stared down at me from every angle - candid shots from events, professional headshots, and even blurry paparazzi images. Scribbled notes with cramped handwriting filled the margins of many articles, but I couldn't make out what they said from where I stood.

My heart sped up. This wasn't just someone interested in celebrity gossip. This was an obsession. I stepped back, my mind reeling as I tried to process what I saw. Why was Eliot so fixated on Sebastian? A sick feeling settled in the pit of my stomach as I realized I had stumbled onto something dark. I should leave this instant, but I didn't. I couldn't tear myself away from the gruesome display.

I cautiously tiptoed toward the wall as if someone would hear me. An old wooden desk, covered in more articles about Sebastian LeClair, sat beneath the massive collage. On top of it all was the picture I found in Sebastian's room. How did that get here? Next to that was an old newspaper article.

BROOKLYN TEEN CRITICALLY INJURED IN FIERY CAR CRASH

Brooklyn Daily Eagle, September 15, 1993

A joy ride turned tragic yesterday when a stolen car crashed and burst into flames on Ocean Parkway, leaving a local teenager fighting for his life. The incident occurred shortly after midnight when the vehicle, reported stolen from a Flatbush residence, lost control and collided with a tree near the parkway.

The teen, whose name is unknown to authorities at this time, suffered severe burns over 40% of his body and is currently in critical condition at Maimonides Medical Center. Doctors say the next 48 hours will be crucial for his survival.

Authorities say only the driver was found at the scene, and they don't know if others are involved.

Authorities remind teenagers of the dangers of reckless driving and the severe consequences of auto theft...

"You just couldn't leave it alone, could you?" he growled from behind me.

I spun around to face a livid Eliot whose lips were curled into a menacing smile while my whole body screamed danger and my mind connected all the pieces. My legs turned to jelly, and my stomach clenched in a terrifying moment of clarity. He was James, Sebastian's and Vincent's friend from the picture, and *he* was the teenager from the burning car.

"You're the third boy in this picture!" I exclaimed, waving it in his direction. "But Vincent told me you died."

"They thought I did. And that's why they took off. They never knew I survived until only recently when I started sending threatening letters to our dear Sebastian LeClair.

"When I woke up in the hospital, I refused to rat them out because I was so sure they'd come for me. But by the time I realized they had taken off, it was too late. They disappeared without a trace, and we were all just nobodies in foster care, so the authorities never bothered to look. No one cared.

"I spent three months in the hospital and then another six months in jail for stealing a car. Can you believe that?

I'm the one who almost died, yet I'm the one who went to jail. And I got these wonderful scars and painful rehab for my loyalty!"

He pulled back his shirt sleeve to reveal an arm full of frightening burn scars. So that's why he was constantly tugging on his shirt sleeves. It also explained the limp.

"That was when I vowed my revenge. I spent my life searching for them, and one day, Lenny appeared on my TV. There was no mistaking that pompous jerk, and I plotted my detailed revenge."

"How did they not recognize *you*?"

"We hadn't seen each other in over thirty years. More importantly, they thought I was dead, so they didn't *expect* to see me."

"I know who you are," I muttered, repeating the note from LeClair's room.

"Yep," he laughed cruelly. "After I started sending him those letters, he announced his retirement and moved here to hide. Or so he thought."

"So, you invented the cover story about writing a book."

"I assure you, it was a long and laborious process."

"But when did you poison the pies? And how?" That was one thing I couldn't figure out. All the contestants were caught in the kitchen at some point, but how did he poison the pies without being caught in the act?

"Lock picking was only one of the useful skills I learned in prison."

"The night before!" I exclaimed. "Sebastian. Or Lenny. Or whatever, saw you in the kitchen and kicked you out!"

Eliot laughed a cruel, hard laugh. "I know! He came this close to catching me. I picked the lock on the fridge, injected all of the pies with poison, and started to head out when that fool saw me and lectured me about being out of bounds. Do you know how much self-discipline it took to stay silent?"

I ignored his boasting about his so called self-discipline. "But why all of them? If you had only injected Juliet's, it would have kept the suspicion on her."

"I had to make sure Lenny ingested enough poison. I never thought one little bite would do it. But I guess he was in such bad health that it was enough."

"But you could have killed the other judges too!" I exclaimed in horror.

"Oh well!" he shrugged. "Hazards of war. If I'm being honest, my original plan was to publicly humiliate him. Oh, how I fantasized about being in the audience when he filmed his show. I pictured myself leaping to my feet and announcing to the world that I knew who Sebastian LeClair really was. But then he had the gall to go and retire! Do you know how angry that made me? Huh? Do you?" he shrieked so intensely, spit flew from his mouth.

"Erm, no?"

"It infuriated me! That's when I decided it wouldn't be enough to humiliate him. I had to kill him."

"What about Vincent?" I asked.

"I couldn't find him anywhere. It's a lot harder when they don't have their own reality show, you know. So, I resigned myself to limiting my revenge to Lenny. But after he died, you can imagine my surprise when Vincent walked right by me on the sidewalk here in Glenwood Springs."

"And then you caught him in Sebastian's room."

"Completely random!" he chortled. "And, even better, I showed up at the hotel the other night, hoping to get lucky with another Vincent sighting, and I did! I got even luckier when I saw him go to Lenny's room. And there was a pie server. It's like it was all meant to be. After I stabbed him, I searched his pockets and came up with one of the notes I had sent Lenny and the picture. Oh, it was glorious! And wasn't he surprised to see me alive!" Eliot laughed.

"Although not as surprised as when I stabbed him. The look on his face right before he died was priceless! This has truly been cathartic," he sighed contentedly, proving just how dangerous he really was. But then his face darkened. "At least it was until you refused to stop poking around. It was one thing to try and outrun the police. They have to follow the rules, but mercy girl, do you get around or what? You're so annoying, you realize that, don't you?"

"That's not the first time I've heard that," I mumbled.

"And let's face it, I've already killed two, what's another one?" He shrugged.

While he talked, I was painfully aware he was blocking the front door. He killed Sebastian and Vincent and laughed about it, and I was next. When his eyes darted to a large knife on the nearby counter, I followed them.

"You sent the wolfsbane to Juliet's bakery!" I exclaimed when it popped into my head.

"But of course! That stupid courier was supposed to arrive while the sheriff was there, but oh no, he had to waste time flirting with some lady outside the bakery, which completely threw off my timing. I even paid extra for it. I was so mad! I should have killed that guy, too. But then I assumed all of you would hide the poison; then I would tip off the authorities, they would go in with a search warrant and bust your friend. But nope! You had to do the right thing and immediately turn it in. Which meant I had to reassess that part of the plan.

"Oh, and by the way, I also called in the unanimous tip about seeing your friend Juliet in the kitchen when she wasn't supposed to be. Unfortunately, I hadn't realized that *all* of the contestants were in the kitchen when they weren't supposed to be. Just goes to show you not everything proceeds as planned, right?' he chuckled as if he was talking about something as mundane as ruining a picnic.

I wanted to keep him talking, to stall for time somehow, but his gaze flickered repeatedly to the knife. In a split second, when his muscles tensed, I knew he was going for it. Without thinking, I grabbed a heavy ceramic vase from the end table beside me. But we moved simultaneously - Eliot diving for the blade, me swinging the vase with all my might.

The vase connected with a sickening thud, and Eliot crumpled to his knees, momentarily stunned. I didn't wait to see if he'd get up. As the pieces of the broken vase fell to the floor, I bolted for the back door, my heart thudding in my ears.

I burst into the overgrown backyard, sprinting for the woods beyond. The trees loomed before me, offering both refuge and uncertainty. Eliot was cursing and stumbling behind me, recovering far too quickly for my liking. He moved much faster than I anticipated for someone who walked with a limp.

With no time to think of an alternative, I plunged into the forest, branches whipping at my face as I ran, Eliot's heavy breathing and shouting not far behind. My only hope was to lose him in the trees and somehow get back to my bus to call for help.

TWENTY-SEVEN
THROUGH THE WOODS

I crashed through the underbrush, branches snagging at my clothes and hair as I fled deeper into the woods. The forest floor was a treacherous maze of exposed roots and fallen leaves, threatening to trip me with every frantic step. My lungs burned as I gulped for air. The taste of fear thickened on my tongue.

"You can't run forever!" Eliot's voice boomed from somewhere behind me, too close for comfort. "I've plotted my revenge for years! Decades! I won't be denied by some two-bit private investigator in a tiny mountain town! I killed Lenny and Vincent without blinking. I'll kill you, too."

His words sent a jolt of adrenaline through me, propelling me forward. I ducked under a low-hanging branch, the rough bark scraping against my forehead, a sharp reminder of the danger I faced.

I tried to quiet my ragged breathing, straining for any sign of Eliot's pursuit. Why were the woods so loud all of a sudden? Every little noise was magnified: the rustle of leaves in the wind, the startled cry of a bird taking flight, the distant gurgle of a stream. Cutting through it all was the unmistakable sound of heavy footfalls and snapping twigs.

"You're just prolonging the inevitable!" he called out, his voice heavy with malice. "Why don't you make it easier on yourself and give up?"

I gritted my teeth, anger flaring alongside my fear. Give up? Not likely. I'd faced down not only killers but childhood bullies on top of that. I wasn't about to let this psychopath win.

As the trees thinned out, I glimpsed a clearing up ahead. Hope surged within me. If I could make it to open ground, maybe I could outpace Eliot and circle back to my bus. I patted my pocket for the keys, just in case. The last thing I needed to do was get back to the bus and not have keys.

But when I finally burst into the clearing, my stomach dropped. It wasn't a way out - it was only a small meadow, enclosed on all sides by more dense forest. All I'd done was run deeper into the woods instead of towards freedom.

"Nowhere to run now!" Eliot's voice rang out again, this time closer than ever. "You're almost making this too easy."

I spun in a circle, frantically searching for an escape route. The trees all looked the same, a bewildering maze of brown and green. Which way had I come from? Which way led back to a road?

I waited too long. Eliot burst through the trees and into the clearing, a wicked grin splitting his face. I couldn't outrun him here. He brandished the knife he'd grabbed from his kitchen, the blade glinting in the sunlight.

I backed away, my mind racing. I needed a weapon, a distraction, anything. There was a thick branch lying a few feet away. It wasn't much, but it was better than nothing.

As Eliot sprinted toward me, I dove for it, my fingers

closing around the rough wood just as he lunged at me. I rolled, then hit my feet, bringing the makeshift weapon up to block his attack. The knife bit into the branch, lodging in the wood.

For a moment, we were locked in a desperate struggle, him trying to wrench the knife free, me trying to use the branch to hit him. My arms shook as I strained against Eliot's strength. His face was inches from mine, contorted with rage and exertion.

"Why couldn't you just leave well enough alone?" he growled. "Sebastian LeClair got what he deserved. Vincent too. They left me to die in that burning car. Then they went on to live their lives like nothing happened. Do you have any idea what that's like? To watch the people who ruined your life succeed while you suffer?"

I realized the accident and his unfortunate childhood had scarred him, inside and out, twisting him into this creature consumed by vengeance. But given that he was trying to kill me, I pushed any pity aside. It wouldn't save me. Only quick thinking and fast feet would.

When he gave up on getting the knife out and tried to pull the branch away from me, I made a split-second decision to let go, throwing him off balance. As he stumbled backward, I brought my knee up hard, catching him in the stomach.

The air left Eliot's lungs in a whoosh, and he doubled over. I didn't waste the opportunity. I backed away from him and ran again. I had to find the stream I heard earlier. Water always led somewhere, and anywhere was better than here.

I sprinted across the clearing, plunging back into the forest, my ears straining for the sound of running water.

Behind me, I could hear Eliot's labored breathing and angry curses as he recovered and resumed the chase.

"You can't escape!" he wheezed. "It's only a matter of time before I catch you!"

Ignoring his taunts, I focused on the terrain ahead. The forest floor sloped downward, and the unmistakable sound of rushing water grew louder. I was on the right track.

But just as I thought I was home free, the ground beneath my feet gave way. I cried out as I slid down a steep embankment, leaves and loose soil cascading around me. I hit the bottom hard, the impact knocking the wind out of me.

I lay on the cold, hard ground, dazed and gasping for air. But the sound of Eliot still after me jolted me back to reality. Ignoring the protest of aching muscles, I scrambled to my feet and realized I had slid down to the bank of a swiftly flowing stream.

The water was shallow but fast, churning over rocks and fallen branches. It wasn't ideal, but what choice did I have? Taking a deep breath and steeling my nerves, I waded into the stream. The icy water shocked my system, but I pushed forward, fighting against the current. Each step was a battle, the slippery rocks threatening to send me tumbling.

"You're only delaying the inevitable!" Eliot's voice rang out from the top of the embankment. "I will find you, and I will finish what I started!"

The water rose to my waist as I struggled to cross the stream, tugging insistently at my body. Every story I'd ever heard on the news about someone getting carried away by a stream they couldn't control crossed my mind.

I glanced back over my shoulder only to see Eliot crashing into the stream, too. What would it take to get away from this guy? He struggled against the current, his face a mask of determination and rage.

What was I thinking by getting in the river? Had I done the right thing? But what else could I do? I wasn't giving in, but the water was bitterly cold, and if I stayed in it much longer, he wouldn't have to kill me; the freezing water would. I struggled forward, sucking in a sigh of relief when I finally reached the other side.

I jogged along the banks of the river, my shoes and pants soaking wet, desperately searching for any signs of civilization. We weren't that far out of town. There had to be someone, somewhere.

When I rounded the bend, my heart leaped. There, in the distance, was a bridge spanning the water. And beyond that, the glint of sunlight on metal - cars! With renewed energy, I pushed forward, ignoring the numbness creeping into my legs as my wet jeans clung to me. Yet just as I thought I'd never get to the road, my feet somehow carried me there, but with Eliot still shouting behind me.

When I heard a car coming, I waved my arms while jumping up and down. I was saved! "Help!" I screamed as I emerged from beneath the bridge. "Somebody help me!" The car laid on its horn, swerved, and kept going. Seriously?

"I hope you step on a Lego!" I shouted as he sped away.

The next car did the same. What the heck? I was begging for my life, and these people acted like I was inconveniencing them. "I hope you run over a nail and get a flat!" I shouted at that one.

But I was so busy casting insults at passing drivers from the middle of the road that I didn't see the one behind me until it was too late. The big black SUV headed straight for me as my heart hammered in my chest and my life flashed before my eyes. I snapped to attention and jumped out of the way while it swerved, slamming on its brakes. At least *they* stopped.

But it wasn't just any SUV. It was from the Sheriff's Department. It was Sheriff Mack!

"Holly! Where have you been? And what are you doing in the middle of the road?"

The story about Eliot being James flowed from my mouth in a rush of mixed-up details and horror. "He was right behind me!" I insisted.

"We've been looking everywhere for you! Get in the car. We'll circle around," Sheriff Mack said as he called in an APB for Eliot.

But before he could finish the call, Eliot crashed through the bushes. "You're dead!" he screamed, a large rock raised high above his head.

"Drop it!" Sheriff Mack commanded, pushing me behind him, and pointing his gun at Eliot.

"Dangnabit!" Eliot swore as he dropped the rock and raised his hands.

Sheriff Mack grabbed Eliot and pushed him against the car. "You're under arrest for the murders of Sebastian LeClair and Vincent and a bunch of other stuff I haven't thought of yet."

In a blink, the area was swarming with law enforcement and paramedics who checked me over thoroughly to ensure I was okay, wrapped me in a blanket, and gave me some dry sweatpants someone found in their patrol car.

I was warming up in the back of an ambulance and enjoying a lively chat with a paramedic when I heard an ear-splitting shriek. "Hollyyyyyyyy!"

Uh oh.

"What in tarnation were you thinkin'?" Juliet scolded, her southern accent thick with fury as she marched straight for me. I'd never seen her so angry or heard her accent so pronounced. "I done told you days ago not to come out here by your lonesome, and here you went and nearly got yourself killed anyway!"

"I just offered to bring a library book to Eliot or James or whatever his name is--" I stuttered. No matter what I said, I didn't think it would be enough.

"And as usual, it almost got you killed!"

"How did everyone find me? Why were you all looking for me anyway?" I responded in utter confusion.

"Remember when I said I'd ask the committee why the pie tasting order was switched?"

"Oh. Yeah. I kind of forgot about that until just now."

"They called me this morning to tell me that Eliot Thornfield was scheduled to go first, but *he* talked them out of it."

"Did they say why?"

"He gave a lame excuse about how someone already well-known within the community should go first. And that was when I realized something was up. I called you, but no answer, so then I called Surly Steve."

"Who's Surly Steve?" Sheriff Mack asked as he came up from behind Juliet.

"Hollyyy!" Wendy shouted as she sprinted for us.

"The gang's all here," Sheriff Mack muttered, shaking his head. "What were you thinking?" he then bellowed at me.

"I was just delivering a library book..." I trailed off. Oh no! The book! I must have dropped it in all the excitement. Would "almost murdered by a homicidal maniac" be an acceptable excuse for losing a library book? I sure hoped so.

"Juliet said she called you," I offered.

"I was already looking for you because we finally caught up to Pastor Greg."

"You did? Did he tell you why he came to my house? Did you tell him that's unacceptable? Killer or not, it was creepy! How did he know all that stuff he shouldn't? Do you know that for a while there, I was sure it was him?" All my jumbled thoughts came spilling out at once.

"He knew all those so-called secrets because one of his parishioners was in the bookstore when you were blabbing to Wendy and Juliet! You have to be more careful. About a lot of things!" he scolded.

"For the record, I didn't realize it was supposed to be a secret when I told them. But still, why show up at my house making veiled threats in the first place?"

"He was worried, given everything you knew, that you'd go public with it and ruin his reputation. He also admitted to missing the Celebration of Life because he was meeting with his lawyers about suing the LeClair estate to get his money back."

"Hmmm. He's still a creep," I insisted.

"I agree, and I told him if I ever caught him pulling a stunt like that again, not only would I arrest him, but I'd go public with it."

"Miss, we need to go now," the paramedic urged me.

"Go? Go where?" Wendy asked.

"They're taking her to the hospital to get checked out," Sheriff Mack insisted.

"I told you, I'm fine," I pleaded.

"Go!" Sheriff Mack yelled.

"C'mon, sweetie, we'll go with you, okay?" Wendy said.

"Uhhh, I'm not supposed to allow that many--"

"Just let them all go," Sheriff Mack said with a wave of his hand. "Trust me, it's useless to argue with them."

"All right, buckle up, ladies, we're going to the hospital."

"You seem like a nice young man," Juliet told the paramedic as Sheriff Mack closed the doors. "Are you single?"

TWENTY-EIGHT
GIVING THANKS

"I got it!" I exclaimed when the doorbell rang.

Mystery, who had been sunning herself in the window, lifted her head. "It's the cops! Run!" she shouted, leaping from the window and sprinting upstairs.

"Happy Thanksgiving!" I proclaimed, throwing open the door.

"Happy Thanksgiving!" Sheriff Mack responded. I had been pondering over what to call him. Steve seemed weird. Mack maybe? His friends often called him Mack.

"Everyone, this is my mom, Iris," he announced.

"Hello!" we all said as we took turns introducing ourselves.

"Oh my," Iris said as she shook my hand. "So you're the young woman with lavender eyes. Stevie talks about you all the time."

Stevie? I mouthed at him behind her back.

"If you ever call me Stevie, I'll lock you up and throw away the key," he hissed at me. "I don't care how much paperwork I have to do. And I don't talk about you. I complain about you."

"Whatever you say," I whispered back.

"Is it true you have ghosts living here?" Iris asked.

I nodded. "I do. And one of them is next to your son right now," I told her, leaving out the part where Clara rubbed his arm, and he shuddered unknowingly from her chilly touch...

THANKSGIVING AT HOLLY'S will be a hoot, and they'll be back with another mystery to solve in January 2025!

ALSO BY B I SKINNER

Ghostly Glenwood Mysteries Paranormal Cozy Mysteries

The Case of the Haunted Hotel

The Case of the Pilfering Poltergeist

The Case of the Poached Peridot The Case of the Gym Ghost

The Peach Cobbler Caper

The Case of the Haunted Radio Station

The Case of the Poisoned Pumpkin Pie

Spooky Shanty Realty Mysteries

Afterlife in the Attic

The Lifeless Listing

Cadaver at the Closing (coming in January)

Holiday Cozy Mysteries (non-paranormal)

Sleigh Bells & Sleuthing

Fireworks & Felons

Marcall's Breakfast Cafe Paranormal Cozy Mysteries

An Eggscellent Day for Murder

24 Carrot Caper

Daggers and Donuts

Cupcakes and Corpses

A Crime of Cranberry

Peppermints & Pandemonium

Star Spangled Homicide Blood Curdling Ballots

Sign up for my email list here

https://mailchi.mp/9ebce0da866a/email-signup-list

Follow me on my personal Instagram **@bethiskinner or** Facebook **@biskinnerauthor**

Cover art by Spellbinding Designs